The Making of a Martyr

The Making of a Martyr

A Novel of . . .
Faith, Bravery and the
Ultimate Sacrifice

(Based on a true story)

by

Robert L. Wise

For
The Archdiocese of Oklahoma
Archbishop Paul S. Coakley

FaithHappenings Publishing
A division of WordServe Literary
7500 E. Arapahoe Rd. Suite 285
Centennial, CO 80112
admin@wordserveliterary.com
303.471.6675

Cover Design: Bouhadda Abderahmane

Interior Book Design: Greg Johnson

ISBN: 978-1-941555-58-3

First Printing, January 2023

Printed in the United States of America

ACKNOWLEDGMENTS

I am grateful to a number of people who followed the career of Father Stanley Rother from the beginning and chronicled the events of his life. Father David Monahan kept an initial account of the unfolding story of the humble priest from Okarche, Oklahoma. Mariá Ruiz Scaperlanda did an extraordinary amount of research in her book THE SHEPHERD WHO DIDN'T RUN. We must forever be grateful for her scholarly composite of the details of Father Rother's ministry.

Archbishop Paul Coakley's dedication to this project has continued to spread the story of the extraordinary ministry of Blessed Stanley Rother. I thank him for his support for this project and for the encouragement he always lends to all. In addition, Archbishop Coakley's administrative assistant Rosemary Lewis has offered gracious help and contributions.

As always, I am indebted for the administrative assistant and editing of Rikki Abrams and Karen Johnson. Thank you for having "keen" eyes.

PREFACE

Blessed Stanley Rother's story is based on fact. Far from a biography, *The Making of a Martyr* contains imaginative elements that nevertheless describe the reality of an era and time of struggle in Guatemala. Some characters are also fictious and products of the author's imagination. Any resemblance to actual persons, living or dead, business, or organization is purely coincidental.

The larger issue is helping readers realize how a faithful man's life changed destinies. The story is art in the quest for the magic that takes one through time, back to the past to a time of adversity when eternity broke through the chaos and transcended the terror and error.

Something about art — even the art of historical narratives like the one you hold in your hands — transcends time magically pulling us away from the pinched present and into a larger realm partaking of eternity. But does not even the taste of eternity make us ache to enter eternity more truly and fully. (pg. xv *Bonhoeffer, Pastor, Martyr, Prophet, Spy*, Eric Metaxas, Thomas Nelson Publishers)

PART ONE
And he called unto himself
a man . . .

1

February 1981

"You know that they will kill you," the archbishop said.

Father Stanley Rother looked down for a few moments. Finally rubbing his calloused hands together, he nodded. "Yes, I know."

The archbishop stared across his large mahogany desk at this man in front of him. At five-feet-ten inches tall, Stanley Rother had the natural handsomeness of a German farmer. On the slender side, Stanley Rother seemed even taller. His neatly trimmed beard and reddish-brown hair framed a sun-tanned kind face.

"I know you realize how volatile the political situation is in Guatemala, Fr. Rother. We keep getting reports that the government remains ruthless. Of course, the rebel groups springing up across the country are equally dangerous. The Church is caught smack dab in the middle. Such an explosive situation makes you an unavoidable target."

The afternoon sunlight poured through the windows, casting shadows over the bishop's office and sending a reflection from the large Crucifix hanging on the side wall. Shelves loaded with books seemed to fade away under the bright light. Outside the cold winds of winter continued to blast against the brick walls. A few flakes of snow bounced against the windows.

Fr. Stanley nodded. "You are correct. The Tz'utujil people that I serve are trapped between a defensive government that cares little for the citizens and rebels who are ready to fight to oust the current regime. Both sides have a great deal to lose."

"And we don't want to lose *you!*" He nervously pulled at the amethyst-purple bishop's ring on his right hand. "We keep receiving communiques that they've put a bullseye on your back. The government knows that you have a highly significant influence on the people. Even though you have nothing to do with politics, the officials fear you. You do understand?"

The priest smiled and shrugged. "I only want to be a good pastor. Lately, I've had to care for families that suffer from malnutrition or have lost their fathers because of murder. In our village half of all children die before they are six years old because of lack of sufficient food. My flock is my primary concern."

The archbishop shook his head. "Yes, yes. We know your heart is pure and your intent is only for the good of the people, but you are dealing with a despotic government. That general who calls himself president wants nothing more than to protect his backside. Ferando Garcia is heartless on a good day, but now that he is threatened there are no lengths that he will not go to protect his position. He sees you as quite expendable."

"Your excellency, I have prayed about this problem unceasingly. Nothing in Guatemala has gotten any better. Yet the church cannot shrink from its responsibility before God. We must support the people and do what we can to protect them."

"Certainly, Father. But we don't want to lose you in the crossfire. That possibility is my prime concern."

"Thank you, your excellency. I do appreciate your care as well as your devotion to the mission cause. I need your prayers every day." Stanley Rother stopped and took a deep breath. "Heaven knows I've prayed without ceasing about the obligations of this missionary work, but I cannot turn my back on my people, especially those of Mayan descent who are despised by the government."

Silence fell over the room. The archbishop leaned back in his chair, folded his hands, and stared at the man sitting in front of him. The elegant cherry wood paneled walls seemed to stand as a silent witness to their conversation. The archbishop ran his hand nervously through his graying hair. He certainly had every reason to believe this might be the last time he would see Stanley Rother and he didn't want it to be so. Stanley had a remarkable devotion to his calling and was good to the core. On the other hand, Stanley had grown up as a German farmer with that natural resoluteness that didn't bend easily. Some would call it stubbornness while others considered him tenacious. The archbishop knew his firmness was much more.

"It's hard to argue with God's purposes," the archbishop finally said. "I suppose that's what I could be doing. The matter is already settled?"

The priest smiled and nodded thoughtfully. "I do believe I have been called to the position I must take. I cannot go off and leave my people behind. Perhaps this is the most critical hour when the natives need to see the Church standing firm ... regardless of the cost."

The archbishop abruptly pounded the desk. "Regardless of the cost? Yes, we could all pay a price. My concern is that you could pay the highest price!"

"I cannot consider the expenditure. I must only remember to be faithful."

A thought abruptly raced through the archbishop's mind, remembering a thousand sermons he had preached asking people to be obedient. The biblical mandates rang through his mind. The commandments were all certainly true, but now they hurt. "Yes," he said slowly. "We all must do what we are called to do."

"I am so called," Fr. Stanley said.

"Then it is settled that you are going back to Santiago Atitlan?"

"I am."

The archbishop leaned forward over his desk and glanced at the old worn icon of St. Luke proclaiming the Word. The fading icon conveyed its own message about faithfulness.

"I admire your convictions more than I can say. While I may not entirely understand the depth of your stance, I want to grasp what makes you so tenacious. Please help me comprehend. Tell me more about what made Stanley Rother become the devoted Father Rother. Tell me more."

The afternoon light faded further, but the archbishop did not move. Fr. Stanley closed his eyes as if he were remembering, remembering the past...

2

Spring 1952

"Stanley!" Gertrude Rother called out the backdoor of their farmhouse. "Stanley, come in here!"

"Mom, he can't hear you with that tractor motor grinding away like a freight train. I'll have to go out to the field to call Stan in."

"Okay, Betty Mae. Go tell that brother of yours to get in here. It's almost supper time."

Betty Mae hurried down the back stairs and walked toward the barbed-wire fence at the back of their grassy yard. Two family dogs fell in, barking as they walked along. Just beyond the fence line red dust blew up behind the tractor cutting furrows across the field where the winter wheat field had once grown. Stanley's Co-op Seed cap appeared pulled down to his ears. As always, he seemed to be lost in his thoughts as he steered the John Deere Tractor down the long rows. Stanley lived in another world while plowing.

Betty Mae had grown up in the quiet predictable world of Okarche, Oklahoma and never thought anything about the occasional strong winter winds or the spring heavy rains. The '50's appeared to be a good time to be living on a farm. America was quiet and predictable. A year behind Stanley in school, she knew the kids all liked her brother and thought of him as a friendly nice guy.

"Stanley!" Betty Mae waved frantically. "Stanley!"

Stanley waved back and the tractor stopped.

"Supper time! Come on in!"

Stan waved his Co-op Seed hat above his head, meaning he was on his way.

Betty Mae laughed. Their father Franz had dropped little Stanley into the big metal driver's seat when he was ten years old. She remembered well worrying that he'd wreck the tractor or fall off, but Stanley immediately drove off like a seasoned farmer. Betty Mae turned back to the house.

Having a couple of out buildings and sheds, the Rother house looked like the rest of the farmers' homes up and down the country road. White with an extended front porch surrounded by a few elm trees, the two-story house had proved a good place to raise four children. With two ropes hanging down from the thick tree limbs, the swing was seldom used now since the children had grown so tall. Still, they let the wind rock the wooden board back and forth while everyone now had their other assignments to help the farm. The house always felt peaceful.

As always, the four children gather around the large dining room table with Franz at one end and Gertrude at the other. With heads bowed, they said together, "Bless us, O Lord, for these thy gifts which we are about to receive from thy bounty. Through Christ our Lord. Amen." The food immediately began being passed around the table. The smell of roast beef blended with the aroma of the brown gravy.

"I'll take some of that corn," brother Tom said.

"Jim," Betty Mae said, "hand Tom the bowl.

"How was school today?" Gertrude asked her children.

"Just an ordinary day," Tom said. "By the way, the students elected Stan as president of the FFA chapter. Not bad for a red dirt farm boy."

"Wonderful," Gertrude said. "We're all proud of you, son."

Franz laid his fork down and rubbed his chin. His eyes narrowed when he focused on Stanley. "Son, what else happened at school today?"

Stanley froze. The questioning tone in his father's voice was all too familiar. He said nothing.

"I hear you were quite busy in chemistry class."

Stanley glanced at the other three children. Smiles had broken out around the table.

"We had a busy class," he said softly.

"The boys down at Aunt Susie's Café had an additional story going round. Your teacher came in and said they nearly had to let the students go home because of the stink that started in the chemistry room."

Stanley dipped into the mashed potatoes and said nothing.

"We heard several boys created that terrible smell," Franz said.

The three other children burst into a muffled laugh.

"Yes, sir," Stanley said. "I was there."

"There indeed!" Franz pointed with his table knife. "I heard they called you into the office and gave you a stern talking to!"

"Yes, sir."

"Down at the café, I heard they gave you a warning."

"Yes, sir."

"Let me remind you where we all came from," Franz said. "In 1893, your great-grandparents moved here from Minnesota. They braved rumors about savage Indians and a barren territory to come and settle in these parts. They were always faithful members of the Church and part of building Holy Trinity Church right here in Okarche. Your mother's people, the Schmitt's, made the same journey from St. Bernard township in Nebraska. They were all good German farmers. Our little town only had about 400 citizens or so in it, but they were all proud of our upbringing. I expect you to uphold that past. Do you understand? I want you to live up to that heritage. That means no more pranks at school."

Stanley kept looking down at his plate.

"Please pass the stink bomb... I mean the roast beef," Jim said.

Tom and Betty Mae burst out laughing.

Franz glared sternly at them. Gertrude kept looking down at her place, trying to hide a smile.

"An interesting thing happened in the assembly at our school today," Stanley said, trying to change the subject. "We had a missionary priest speak."

"I think he was from India," Betty Mae added.

"Father George Martin was his name I believe," Stanley said. "He told us about what they were doing for the native people and helping them learn how to farm more profitably. I had no idea everyone wouldn't know about taking care of the land. Apparently, they didn't. Can you imagine a priest helping with the farming?"

"Many of us went through a similar hard time in the '30's during the Dust Bowl days," Franz said. "Had a mighty hard struggle back them. Sure. A knowledgeable priest could make a big difference."

"Well, this Fr. Martin not only says Mass for them, but he works alongside the people in the fields. I find that impressive." Stanley glanced at his father, hoping the school prank was no longer discussable. "You know, I've never been out of the United States. Hardly out of Oklahoma. I bet India would be a fascinating place to see."

Betty Mae glanced at him with a slight smile. She knew what he was trying to do.

"Do you like those green beans?" Gertrude asked. "We canned them last summer."

"Oh, yes," Tom said.

"Fine supper," Stanley said. "If I might be excused, I have some schoolwork to do."

"Yeah, like studying chemistry," Jim said.

"You may leave the table," Franz said. "But don't forget that the whole family is going to say Compline tonight before we go to bed. Some of us might need to be asking for a little forgiveness." Stanley gulped and pushed away. Betty Mae kept grinning at him.

3

Fall 1952

The ominous heat of August cooled as September rolled in. The 100° days slid down into the nineties and lower. The wheat had been cut back in June and the fields plowed in preparation for the fall. Cattle still grazed on the back acres while the farm families got ready for the State Fair. Always held in September, the exhibits and show animals were part of the sprawling midway which offered everything from throwing baseballs at wooden milk bottles to rides that whirled visitors around until they were dizzy. People poured in from across the state. Stanley Rother and his friend Bob Jenkins were no exception.

"Look at 'em new Fords," Bob said as they walked through the long exhibition hall filled with the latest cars.

"Yeah," Stanley answered. "And that big Buick knocks your eyes out. Really something to see."

"Yeah. Compared to our worn pickup trucks for sure." Jenkins pointed to the exit door. "Let's go outside and walk toward the rides."

"Maybe we'll see a cotton candy booth. I love that sweet stuff."

The boys meandered through the crowd of strollers walking from building to building. High school kids their age mingled among old ladies coming out of the cooking exhibition. Several young couples strolled by hand-in-hand. Stanley and Bob kept walking toward the large archway holding the big sign, "Fun Time," in large red letters. On the far side they could see a large Ferris Wheel giving screaming and hollering kids a long circular ride with an overview of the city. Inside a huge tank, motorcycle riders were already riding around and around while the visitors watched their dangerous stunts.

The two boys walked along, taking it all in like they had never seen such entertainment before.

"Here it is!" a side show roustabout called out. Dressed with an old time flat-topped straw hat and a striped vest, he yelled, "Bust a balloon and win a Teddy bear. You two gentlemen! Here's a chance to take home a prize for your girlfriends!"

The boys laughed and kept walking.

"Step right up!" the amplified voice echoed across the sideshow lot. "Here's what you've come to see! Straight from Paris, France. We've got the hottest women in the world."

The boys stopped and stared. On a large, raised platform, a fat man screamed into a microphone and looked down on the group gathering in front of the stage. Behind him stood three women in short flashy costumes looking enticing. Stanley thought they looked something far less than the promotion. With gaudy glaring lipstick and long false eyelashes, they looked on the hard side.

"Come on down men. Meet Fee-Fee." He stopped. "I mean Madame Mosel ... er ... whoever. These dancing girls want to show you much more, but you've got to come inside the tent to see their show. Normally, you'd pay $25 in Paris, but we have a special today. No, not even $5 to look," he chuckled, "And I *mean to look* at these women to say the least. Step right up. Step closer."

Bob Jenkins grinned at Stanley. "Man alive. We can't let this go by."

"We're about to open the tent," the barker yelled. "You men come on down and walk up these steps. Sorry. No children or ladies allowed. Because today is Monday, we're only charging fifty cents for the show of a lifetime. The girls are waiting for you to come on in."

"Let's go!" Bob Jenkins said. "We've each got fifty cents. Come on."

The crowd of men began climbing the steps. Bob and Stanley fell in. The boys started up the stairs. The barker kept promising a girly show like no other. Halfway up Stanley glanced at the line forming behind them. Standing at the far edge of the crowd was a man in a black suit with a white clerical collar staring at them.

"On no!" Stanley gasped. "Father Von Elm is over there watching us!"

Bob Jenkins looked. "Got to get out of here!"

The boys turned and pushed back down the steps, winding their way through the crowd behind them. Once they blended into the crowd, they made sure that Father Von Elm couldn't see them.

"Do you think he saw us?" Bob Jenkins asked.

"Are you kidding? Of course, he did."

"Well, so much for the girly show."

The boys drifted off toward the barns where the prize cattle were kept.

***

The bell rang for early morning classes. Stanley was coming down the hall when he noticed Father Elm coming up the steps. He nodded respectfully.

"Saw you at the State Fair," Fr. Von Elm said.

"Oh? Well … we always look at the prize exhibits and the animals."

"Did you know? So, I noticed." Fr. Von Elm raised an eyebrow. "We have a special priest coming here from China. Fr. Boesmans was expelled by the new Communist regime. I know your family always provides a wonderful meal, especially for our guests. You think your parents would be up for it tonight?"

"I'm sure," Stanley said. "You could call my mother. I know she'd like the idea."

"I'll do that immediately." The priest turned and walked away.

Stanley smiled. At least, the good Father knew how to keep a secret.

***

Betty Mae rushed into the kitchen. "He's here, mother. And he's in there talking to father and Stanley. Father Von Elm came also. The boys are listening. We've got to hurry and get everything on the table."

"What's his name again?" Gertrude asked.

"Boesmans. He was originally from Belgium."

"Betty Mae put that bowl of salad on the table and call the men in to sit down."

One look at the table said it all. There was hardly room for anymore large items in the array of food across the table.

"We're ready," Betty Mae called. "Please come in and take a place."

Franz Rother took his usual place at the head of the table. Stanley sat across from the guest and everyone else fell in. Father Von Elm sat at the opposite end. As always, the family said the blessing together and then began passing the food.

Gertrude asked, "We understand that the Chinese expelled you along with many other ministers. What happened?"

"China is going through a terrible upheaval," Fr. Camille Boesmans said. "Communism had taken over the government. I'm afraid the Christian faith is being tragically suppressed. Missionaries are seen as agents of the West and Imperialism. The great work of people like St. Francis Xavier has been pushed underground."

"You were there a long time?" Stanley asked.

"Long enough." Fr. Boesmans said. "I will miss the people something terribly. They were my friends as we worked together. They called our faith 'Religion of the Lord of Heaven.' The Chinese were most dear to me." He silently looked down at his plate. "Most dear indeed."

"Just think about all that was lost when they ran you out," Stanley said.

"Oh no!" Fr. Boesmans's reserved countenance abruptly changed. "Missionaries have left an indelible imprint on China. We have helped countless numbers find new life and hope. That is to say nothing about how we helped their economy and farming. We have been faced with a momentary setback, but our impact will arise on another day. We taught the people to worship and find the power of the Eucharist. That can never be taken away."

"Never!" Father Von Elm added.

"Interesting." Stanley leaned back in his chair. "Very interesting."

"The missionaries have sown seeds that will sprout in another time. I cannot imagine giving my life for anything more valuable than spreading the seeds of eternity."

"Is missionary work hard?" Stanley asked.

"My son, remember that no matter the physical cost, the work of the Kingdom is always light."

"Most helpful," Betty Mae said. "You give us something important to think about."

4

April 1953

The sound of the organ playing the final hymn echoed in the background as the church doors opened. Stanley had started out the back from Holy Trinity Church's daily mass when a gust of cold wind stung his face. He flinched but noticed a teacher standing just down the steps.

"Well Stan," Sister Clarissa Tenbrink said. "How are you?"

"Sister Clarissa! Good to see you."

"Only seems like yesterday when you were in my fifth- grade class. Now look at you. You've grown so tall. I hear you're about to graduate this Spring."

Stan grinned. "Time sure does move fast."

"They tell me you're the president of the FFA."

"Yes, Sister." He shrugged.

"You've done very well," Sister Clarissa said. "What will you do next year?"

"Oh, I've been thinking about several things. Of course, I always help the family out there on the farm."

"Stan, I particularly noticed you when you were in my fifth-grade room. You were a nice boy who smiled a lot, but I saw something more. I believed that God had a special plan for your life."

Stanley swallowed hard. "Really?" He shrugged. "Oh, I'm just a farm boy."

"I think you have a destiny. Nothing wrong with being a farmer. Nothing at all. But I sense a different kind of calling on your life."

He blinked several times. "I don't know. I guess I'm still thinking about it all."

"I want you to know that I'm standing behind you 100 percent. I want to encourage you to look beyond what you might have thought possible. Society desperately needs young men with higher and noble ambitions. The church continues to look for people who can make the world better. Stan, the Lord can use you in ways that you never imagined."

"Sister, I don't know what to say. I always took whatever you told us seriously. I'll give some thought to your suggestions. I certainly will."

"If you need me, don't hesitate to call," Sister Clarissa said. "I do believe that God has his eye on you." She patted him on the arm. "God bless you, Stan."

He watched her walk away and then turned back to re-enter the church. A few people were still kneeling in the pews. The lights were low with an intense focus on the altar. The stained-glass windows spread red, blue, and yellow beams across the entire sanctuary. Stan looked around at the beatific scene and thought about the Sister's words. He began to experience an inner churning, a slight glow in his chest. Something seemed to be moving within. He wasn't sure, but the impact was felt.

Dropping on the kneeler, Stan leaned forward and started to pray.

***

Spring had come once again, sending up the irises and tulips. The leaves returned to the barren tree limbs, and the grass turned from brown to green. When the heavy rains came pouring down, the promise of summer remained not far ahead. The wheat began turning yellow and harvest would be just around the corner. The Rother's recognized this year would be different. Stanley was a day away from graduating and Betty Mae would begin her senior year in the Fall. Change would certainly be blowing in the wind this Spring.

As always, the family began supper with the usual prayer they always said. Food started passing from hand to hand around the table. Gertrude poured iced tea into each person's tall glass. "Thought we'd have a change tonight," she said. "Instead of water or milk we'll have some nice cold iced tea in honor of Stan's achievement."

"What's so special?" Tom said.

"Don't give me that," Berry Mae fired back. "You know Stan's graduation is tomorrow."

"Graduation?" Tom feigned a frown. "Don't believe I've heard of that before."

Jim started laughing. "Well, graduation is just like the day before we start butchering. Before you know it, steak is on the way."

"Stop it," Betty Mae said. "We all know graduation is an important time."

"Hard to believe Stanley will be done with high school," Franz said. "Time sure has whizzed by."

"Why, just yesterday I was enrolling you in Holy Trinity grade school," Gertrude said, "And here we are now on the jumping off place."

"I guess that's a good way to say it," Betty Mae said. "The jumping off place means significant change. I think the time has come to tell you what I am planning to do."

Franz laid his fork down on the plate. "What do you mean, Betty Mae?"

She took a deep breath and bit her lip. "I've been thinking about this for a long time and as Spring approached, I knew I had to decide. You understand that it hasn't been easy."

"What are you talking about, dear?" Gertrude frowned.

"I have decided to forgo my senior year here. I want to go to Wichita, Kansas and join the Sisters of the Adorers of the Blood of Christ. I want to become a nun."

Silence fell over the table. Gertrude covered her mouth with her hand. Franz froze in his chair. The brothers stared.

"All these years, the Sisters from this convent have been my teachers. Their example has inspired me, and I can't imagine anything better than to be like them. That's what I want to do with my life." She looked down at the tablecloth. "I don't know what else to say. I can finish my senior year with the Sisters and then prepare to serve just as they do. I guess that's all I can say."

Franz sat immobile. Gertrude got up and walked around the table to hug her daughter. Thirteen-year-old Jim kept blinking his eyes. Tom sat silent.

"We're mighty proud of you, my dear," Franz broke the silence. "Of course, we're surprised, but grateful you want to give your life serving God.

"I don't know how I'll ever dig up potatoes without you," Tom said. "We always did that together."

Everybody laughed and the tension eased. Gertrude sat back down. The family quietly absorbed what Betty Mae had just told them.

"I guess we'll have to drive you up to Wichita to the convent," Franz said.

Betty Mae only nodded. Tears filled her eyes. Quiet returned.

"I suppose it's now my turn," Stanley said. "I've been giving lots of thought to what comes next. Always assumed it would be farming, but lately I've been thinking in a different direction. Hasn't been easy to come to a decision, but I think I have." He smiled at his parents. "I've decided to go to seminary and become a priest."

Franz and Gertrude looked like lightning had struck.

"Y-you what?" Gertrude stammered.

"I believe I should become a priest of the Church."

Gertrude closed her eyes and her head dropped. "This is more than a mother can take," she mumbled quietly. "I'm losing my two oldest children at the same moment. "Oh, my, my."

Everyone sat in stunned silence.

"I've been thinking about St. John's Seminary in San Antonio. I know they take candidates right out of High School."

"Son, we're all surprised," Franz said slowly. "Just assumed you'd go into farming full time. But we're proud. Mighty proud. The family is behind you all the way. God bless you, Stan."

"It's just that I'll be losing two children at the same time," Gertrude said. "How will we ever endure?"

"We'll find a way," Franz said. "God will provide a new path. We've been blessed with two wonderful children. Now the time has come for them to leave and make the world a better place. I'm thankful that they were with us this long."

Stanley looked at his sister. Her name would be changed to fit her calling and his future would be different from anything he had previously imagined. Maybe Sister Clarissa knew what she was talking about. Maybe, there was an unexpected destiny out there for them after all.

5

Winter 1954

The crisp days of Autumn slowly blended into winter as Halloween gave way to Thanksgiving. Leaves tumbled down over people's yards and filled their flower beds now empty of summer's bright flowers. Blustery winds of winter blew snow across Oklahoma's red dirt but did not drift further south into San Antonio. In the city of the Alamo, old San Antonio's diverse population had grown into a metropolis. Begun as a Spanish mission and colonial outpost in 1718, the village became the first chartered civil settlement in 1731, back in the days of the Spanish Empire. Run by the Vincentian Fathers, today's St. John's Seminary hugged the past with eyes on the future as it welcomed high school graduates beginning their training for the Roman Catholic priesthood. Stanley Rother entered as a naïve, reserved, modest student with high hopes.

With the first hint of a sunrise, the chapel bells tolled the beginning of the new day. The long, somber sound pushed the students out of bed. Following the rules of the seminary, Stanley Rother fell into bed every night at 10:00 and got up at the required 5:30 with the first ringing of the bells. Early morning Mass, breakfast, and classes kept him focused on what the new day brought. Unexpected challenges immediately demanded more academically than he expected from high school. However, others noticed that Oklahoma farm life had drifted in with him.

"I've been following your progress," the Rector said. "I noticed that you are adhering to our disciplines well. You are to be commended."

"Thank you." Stanley nodded politely.

"However, I discovered that you struggle with Latin," the Rector frowned. "Is that so?"

"I'm afraid languages are a real challenge," Stanley said. "Latin is particularly difficult."

"Yes," the priest pursed his lips. "Of course, Latin is basic to your calling and highly important. You must try harder." He shuffled through a file on his desk. "I see that you grew up as a farm boy. Worked hard on the land, did you?"

"Oh, yes sir. I'm used to hard work."

"Hmm," the Rector smiled. "Maybe you just need a little more exercise. Perhaps a change of pace could help." He glanced out the window. "We've been needing to put in some new shrubs across the front of this building. Is that the kind of work you've been used to doing during your farming days?"

"No problem with that project. Yeah, I know how to plant your bushes. When do you want me to start?"

"How about late this afternoon after your last class?"

"That will work. Where will the plants be?"

"I'll make sure that a truck sets them along the curb. We certainly appreciate your efforts."

"Glad to help the seminary any time."

"Good! Excellent. See you this afternoon."

The Rector watched his student leave. He said to himself "That's a strong looking young man. Useful."

***

Stanley looked at the line of buckets sitting on the curb. The boxwood shrubs were large along with each holder filled with a good load of dirt. The cool winter weather made carrying the heavy buckets somewhat easier, but each container certainly proved heavy enough. Stanley picked up the shrubbery in each arm, carrying two at a time. Leather gloves kept the heavy rims from cutting into his hands. Setting the two pots down in the empty flower bed, he returned to pick up two more. Back and forth, back and forth, he trudged across the campus, lugging the pails.

Picking up a large shovel, he began digging the holes. The ground seldom froze in San Antonio, but the soil felt dry and hard. Nevertheless, Stanley kept plugging away. A cold blast sent a sharp taste of winter across the campus. Without flinching, Stanley continued placing each shrub the prescribed distance from the others.

The Rector watched from the administrator's window and turned to his assistant. "I tell you what. That Stanley Rother may not be good in Latin but he's an A+ study in hard work. We need to keep that boy busy."

Stanley finished planting the last shrub. The row looked precise, prime, and proper. Dusting off his shovel, he took off his leather gloves and wiped his forehead. He glanced down the long row. "Looks good," he said to himself. "But I sure wish I'd been up there studying Latin."

***

The instructor walked back and forth in front of the young students. Stanley leaned forward to catch each word. The gray-haired old man stopped and pointed at the class. "You will face the challenge! Maybe not in this decade or the next, but slowly the infiltration will shift across this country. People won't notice the shift because they will absorb the idea uncritically, but the impact will be the same."

What's he talking about? Stanley wondered. *Never heard such a suggestion back there in Okarche.*

"Some of you do not consider philosophy to be particularly significant, but you will soon begin to see this idea working its way into movies, into television. Probably, the shift will begin in the thinking of young people. The Church will be challenged. So, you must be aware of what is ahead."

Stanley raised his hand. "I don't understand. What is this 'it' you are speaking of?"

"Secularism!" The teacher waved his fist in the air. "Secularity will turn people's eyes only on this world, not to eternity. Humanity will be elevated to the position of divinity. People will think they no longer need God because they will believe they can achieve all things without divine assistance. Secularism will pronounce the Church to be irrelevant!"

Stanley dropped back in his seat. Never had he dreamed of such an idea. How could this professor know?

"I have spent a lifetime following ideas," he continued. "Earlier philosophers began rejecting the idea of an objective evil and then they carried the thesis of humanism even further. Logical Positivism elevated human reasoning to a level that rejected the supernatural as superstition. The world became flat again with no horizon left but empty space. This ideology is that of what I speak."

The class sat silent. Stanley stared.

The buzzer rang. "You are dismissed." The professor turned away.

Stanley slowed gathered his notebook and class syllabus. Feeling like he was in shock, he trudged out of the classroom.

One of the Vincentian Fathers stopped Stanley in the hall. "Mr. Rother, I have a copy of your grades from the last term." He handed him an envelope. "Here they are." The priest rolled his eyes and walked away.

"What did you get," Joseph Parsons asked.

Stanley looked at the friend he'd made during the preceding semester. Joseph had proved to be an understanding guy who Stanley knew was a good student. He might not be sympathetic with what he suspected his grades would be.

"I'm afraid to look in the envelope."

Joseph laughed. "Come on. Can't be that bad."

"I've really had to struggle with Latin and logic. I know I'm near the bottom of the class." He tore open the envelope and pulled out the small slip of paper. "Just as I feared."

"Tell me," Joseph said.

"I got a C- in Latin and a D- in logic." Stanley squinted and gritted his teeth. "Just what I feared."

"Oh, no!" Joseph patted him on the shoulder. "So sorry."

"I've worked so hard."

"Yeah, and you've put in plenty of time helping run this place. I saw you carrying those large boxes of books up the stairs to the rector's office. Stan, you are really strong."

"They don't give me grades for helping out with the work around here. I feel like my boat is sinking. I also got a D- in English. Language is tough for me.

Joseph pointed to the paper. "But you got an A in religion. That's no small accomplishment."

"I have studied hard," Stanley said. "You know sometimes I don't feel well from all this stress. It's getting to me physically. I think my struggles are hurting my body."

"Look," Joseph said. "Shiner, Texas is my hometown. Not far from here. Why don't you take some time off and come home with me for the weekend? Put your feet up. Don't worry about your classes. Just lean back and take it easy. A little time out might do more for your grades when you come back. Why not?"

Stanley rubbed his forehead. "That's an interesting idea. Maybe I should take a break."

6

Shiner, Texas had been around for quite a while. In 1885, a post office called Half Moon was opened at a trading post near where Shiner stands today. In 1887, an old cowboy named Henry B. Shiner donated 250 acres for a depot and right-of-way for the San Antonio and Aransas Pass Railway which bypassed Half Moon. Because the new train roared through Shiner's donated land, the town grew up around the railroad tracks and his name stuck. Before long you have a cohesive Czech community developing after the German community. And German immigrants became the dominant residents, but Shiner also developed a cohesive Czech community that still heavily influences the town. Of course, ranching was key to the town's history. Cowboy hats and boots remained the order of the day.

In time Shiner became the home of the Spoetzl Brewery, the oldest independent brewery in Texas. The brewery is most well known for producing Shiner Bock, a dark German/Czech-style beer distributed all over America. With a population of 2,180 citizens and 79 households, Shiner was small enough for everybody to know all about everybody down to the last dog sleeping on the steps of the city hall. In the center of town, St. Cyril and Methodius Catholic

Church stands as a testimony to the faith of the people who built the community. Joseph Parsons had grown up there and felt the call to priestly service while sitting within those hallowed walls.

Around town one hears lots of "Ya' alls" or an invitation to dinner might be, "Ya' come now, ya hear?" Joseph grew up wearing a cowboy hat and speaking that South Texas dialect. Men were generally called "boys" and women "gals." No one meant anything by it. Just the local lingo.

"Here we are." Joseph pulled up his car in front of an old white two-story house. "Grew up in one of those upstairs rooms. My family's been here forever. Come on in and meet my mother."

Probably built somewhere around the 1920's, the Parson home looked like it could use a new coat of white paint. Red geraniums were planted in large ceramic pots sitting on the edge of the front steps. An old wooden swing hung from chains fixed to the top of the porch. The home imparted a homey inviting feeling.

The front door swung open before the young men got to the porch screen. A heavy-set woman wearing an apron rushed out. "Joseph! My boy! You're home." Anna Parsons hugged her son and planted a warm kiss on his cheek. "Who do we have here with you?"

"Stanley Rother is a fellow seminarian, Mother. One of my classmates."

"Well, my goodness! Special indeed. Ya' all come in."

Anna Parsons acted like the visit was a big surprise when she knew all about it along with Stanley Rother coming. She knew he was an Oklahoma boy. Being a big University of Texas football fan, she knew they'd have to discuss the Fall big game sooner or later. Better later.

"You boys put up your things and then come on down. I'll finish fixin' supper. Have I got a surprise for you, but that'll wait 'til we finish eatin'. Go on up." Joseph showed Stanley to the guest room.

The guest room proved to be decorated in early '30s rodeo style with horses all over the wallpaper, but the bed was comfortable. The chest of drawers looked like furniture from an earlier century and the pictures on the walls were of fields of Texas blue bonnets. Stanley settled in and stretched out on the bed. Shiner, Texas certainly felt like a good place to take it easy and for a few hours get away from the seminary grind. Stanley stretched out on the bed and closed his eyes. He was immediately in dreamland.

"Ya' all come on down," Anna Parsons called up the stairs.

Stanley woke with a start.

"Suppers ready. The steaks is hot and ready for you boys to dig in."

Stanley hopped off the bed and came down to the dining room. A large room with a long wooden table, the ceiling had a sparkling chandelier that reflected a by-gone day. "Now, Joseph you're our family priest-to-be. You say the blessing."

The prayer was the same one the Rothers said Stanley joined in under his breath.

"Have I've got a surprise for you," Anna said. "The American Legion is throwing a shindig tonight down at the Legion Hall. Gonna' be quite a dance. I got tickets for you boys to attend."

Joseph start laughing. "My mother always covers all the bases. Stan, she's already planned a big evening for you."

***

Hardly a decade after World War II, the American Legion Hall reflected constant use by the returning soldiers, but now streamers had been hung from the ceiling and the bright lights replaced with red and blue bulbs that transformed the expansive wooden floor into a dancing hall. Stanley and Joseph found a table and sat down to watch the show. Couples were already dancing.

"They serve lots of cokes because most of the kids will be high school age" Joseph explained. "The chaperones police the punch bowl but some of the boys always try to smuggle in a little booze to pour in when nobody is looking. That's the challenge of the evening."

Stanley laughed. "Almost sounds like home."

The music started up with the record player blasting out one of the '50s favorites, The Monotones singing "The Book of Love." More teenagers merged out on the floor and the party was on full steam ahead. The mood heightened the space when "At the Hop" picked up the pace. Two girls walked toward the table.

"Joseph, where you been?" the tall, thin girl asked. "Haven't seen hide nor hair of you since the last school year."

"Sally Randolph! Hey, I went off to school," he answered.

"I'll tell you what. It's time for you and your friend to join the party. Let's dance, Joseph."

"Hi, I'm Mary Lou Bartlett," the pretty little girl said to Stan. "I like to dance. Will you join me?"

Stanley looked around. Such was unexpected. He'd planned only on being a spectator. "Well, I guess." He slowly got out of his chair.

"Here we go," Mary Lou took his hand. "Let's cut a rug."

Stanley laughed but glided into the beat of "Let the Good Times Roll." The new rock-and-roll tempo with drums beating out the loud new bop style and sent couples whirling across the dance floor. The record player next sent the Big Bopper's "Chantilly Lace" sailing across the room. The new rock and roll step swept away the old two-step style for good. Stanley danced a couple more times with Mary Lou and then beat a retreat. The evening proved to be a highly charged alternative to the somber sound of the seminary's chapel bells. By 11:00, he and Joseph left the still rocking Legion Hall. The evening had truly been a diversion.

***

"You've found Shiner to be a good place to put your feet up and let the world go by?" Joseph asked. "You were out there on the dance floor like an old pro. Letting your hair down."

Stanley laughed. "Far from it, but I did dance a little back in Okarche. I noticed the girls sure seem to like to dance with guys they don't even know. I wasn't expecting that experience."

Joseph laughed. "I think that's the new style. Girls even dance with each other. It's sort of 'go out there and gyrate.' I want you to see our parochial school that's over there by St. Cyril and Methodius Church. We should find some clerics to wear when we walk through. Be good for the locals to know me in my new status as a seminarian. A few might even be surprised."

"Okay. I'll put on a collar and my black suit. You ready to go?"

"Sure, I'll drive us over there."

The tour of Shiner had to be short and sweet since there wasn't that much territory to cover down a few narrow streets. A swing by the Spoetzl Brewery proved to be the highlight that took about two minutes before they pulled up in front of the school.

"Nuns from San Antonio generally teach here," Joseph said. "Nice people. I probably still know a few of the teachers. Just nod to them when you walk by. They'll get a kick out of seeing me dressed like an honest to goodness cleric."

They got out of the car and walked up the sidewalk. The school was a flat roofed building decorated with shrubbery on all sides and well kept. They swung the double doors open and walked in. The entry hall began to fill with students as they changed classes. Just typical kids with books and notepads in their arms. Most of the teenagers looked inquiringly at them as they passed by. Some smiled; some stared; some paid no attention.

"See anybody you know?" Stanley asked.

"Just kids. Most were younger when I was here."

"Holy Toledo!" A girl yelled. "It's them!"

Stanley looked over his shoulder. The girl named Sally Randolph was standing by the drinking fountain. Next to her was Mary Lou Bartlett.

"Those are the two guys we danced with last night!"

"Heaven help us!" Mary Lou shrieked. "They are holy Joes!"

Students turned and stared at the two seminarians.

"Good Lord, they've turned into priests!" Sally said loud enough that everyone could hear.

Joseph waved feebly. "Keep walking. Don't stop."

Stanley picked up the pace. "I think I want to find the back door.

7

Stanley's break in Shiner had been positive and he felt better. Joseph Parsons had been right. A little time away from the books had been a relief. Of course, his struggles with Latin and Logic remained and he knew the difficulties had to be faced. Perhaps, he could study harder, although he didn't see how. Today's class in Religion was one where he always did well. Stanley flipped the pages in his notebook.

The professor cleared his throat and opened a Bible. The class became silent. "Today I want you to notice the fourth chapter of Matthew's Gospel. You will note that Jesus is both filled with the Holy Spirit and immediately confronted by the Evil One. Beginning seminarians do well to observe the struggle we find in this chapter. Fundamentally, Jesus was being tested to reject his calling as the Messiah."

Stanley thought about his own struggles. Could that be a way in which he was being tried?

"The issue you must face is that your calling will be examined and confronted just as Jesus's was. Evil will attempt to divert you from your holy tasks.

Stanley took a deep breath. The question was personal.

"Each of you will find many subtle ways in which your vocation is tried. If Jesus faced extreme moments, do you think it will be any easier for you?" The professor walked around in front of the podium. "Sin comes in many forms and is always an issue. Of course, you must constantly visit the Confessional to repent of such sins when they come. However, the most subtle form often occurs when you question your own ability to perform the tasks of ministry. Some will find being celibate a challenge when you must live in solitude. At other times, the sheer pressure of constant work may drag you down. My point is that you must live in this fourth chapter of Matthew until you emotionally and personally understand what Jesus faced because you will face the same."

The words sunk deeply into Stanley's thinking. The seminary had certainly been more difficult than he expected. His studies demanded everything he had in him. Latin seemed impossible to master. Could his courses become a demonic distraction from what he had believed back in Okarche? Living as a celibate had not seemed too great a load to carry but it was a task. Certainly, he had sought the help of the Holy Spirit. Yes, the struggle to deal with difficult subjects could certainly become a real distraction from his calling. He had to give a firm no to that temptation.

"You will note that this section of scripture ends by Jesus refusing to yield and rejecting the Evil One," the teacher said. "He did so by renouncing him and saying, 'Worship the Lord God, and serve Him only.' That is the answer you must remember and emulate. Do not be distracted by your struggles! Let any problem lead you to greater worship and adoration of our Lord. That is where you will find the answer that you will need."

I must remember this insight. Stanley began scribbling in his notebook. *Yes, I needed to hear this today. I must keep this lesson before me regardless of the cost or the struggle. God help me.*

***

Joseph Parsons ran into Stanley outside the classroom as the seminarian's exchanged rooms for the next subject and lecture. "How did it go today?"

"An important lecture," Stanley answered. "I need to remember what I heard."

"Good. Don't worry about the pressure."

"Easy for you to say. You are a top of the ladder student."

` "You just need to take a breather more often. Helps you not worry so much. Did you ever wander through the mission remains of *Nuestra Senora de La Purisma Concepetión de Aculna* that the locals call Mission Concepcion? That would be a good exercise for you."

"Never heard of it."

"Quite a history. Way back in 1716, the Spanish founded the place partly because they were concerned that the French might invade the area. The missionaries who ran the site struggled with serious problems in their attempts to convert the local Indians. You'd find it fascinating."

"Interesting. Maybe I can run over there this afternoon. I'll see."

"Hang in there, Stan. You'll do okay."

Immediately following lunch, Stanley had one more class. English. Oooh—his worst. It wasn't that he didn't understand, but that he had no disposition for the subject. What Stanley had brought with him from high school didn't help much. English felt boring to a farm boy and now he was paying the price for not paying better attention. Stan knew he had to study doubly hard. When the class ended, he returned to his room. Sitting on the bed, he remembered Joseph's suggestion to visit *Nuestra Senora de La Purisma Concepetión de Aculna.* Maybe a walk through the mission would in some way bring restoration.

What he had learned of the mission was the history of a struggle between the missionaries and the secular Spanish authorities. At some point the Fathers moved the Mission Concepcion closer to the San Antonio River

When he walked onto the restored grounds, Stan stared at the towering steeples on each side of the ancient building worn by the three centuries of wind and ran. To one side, a flat roofed wall extension from the sanctuary carried the gray- black stains that the year had splotched over the entire structure. Stanley walked up to the steeple above the large front entrance constructed like an old Spanish door with beams and planks tied together with large brads and steel ornaments beaten into the heavy wood. Time had only made the entry seem more sacred. He walked in.

A small pamphlet explained that the mission of the first priests was to reach the Pajalat, Tacame, Siquipil, Tilpacopal, Patumaca, Patalca, and Coahuiltecan groups. The Fathers had made an impact through times of struggle, sickness and dark days. Their work had transformed the entire countryside from which San Antonio was to spring. The times had been difficult, but the faithfulness of those early missionaries had produced a completely new way of life extending to this very day.

Inside the lights had been turned on along the long knave. The smell of candle wax filled the air. Obviously refurbished over the years, the simplicity of the church pointed to the altar at the front where a large picture of the risen Christ in glory seemed to reach out and touch the observer. While not ornate, the sanctuary felt saturated with prayer from hundreds of people making intercession for their pain and needs over the centuries.

For a long time, Stanley thought about the missionary enterprise represented by this church. Simple people had profoundly changed the world. Could there be any greater calling? He didn't think so. Slowly, Stanley got out of the pew and walked back to the front door. Maybe Latin was more important than he had realized.

8

Spring 1959

The Rector sat at his second-story desk staring out the window. The seminary rector could see Stanley Rother planting flowers in the beds and removing dead stems and withered leaves the winter winds had left behind from last Fall. Always hard-working, Stanley had certainly proved an asset for tasks that no one else performed around the seminary. The Rector remained keenly aware of how valuable Stanley had been to him, carrying up heavy boxes and taking care of details no one else touched. He certainly was a strong lad.

"Father Randolph!" The rector called in a robust demanding voice that made people jump. "Bring me that file on Stanley Rother in here."

The assistant administrator hurried in. "Yes. Everything is up to date." He handed the administrator a vanilla-colored file. "Anything else?"

"That will do for the moment." The Rector opened the file and quickly surveyed the notations. "Just as I was afraid," he mumbled to himself. "Not good." He looked out the window again and shook his head. "He failed the first semester and can't begin to read the textbooks in Latin. He just hasn't done enough." He shook his head again. "We will miss Stanley. Such a nice guy." He roared, "Father Randolph! Get Father Kavanaugh in here!"

"He simply can't get hold of Latin," the seminary rector kept mumbling to himself as he drummed on the desk with his fingernails. "Just too bad."

Father Thomas Kavanaugh appeared in the doorway. "You called?"

"Oh yes." The Monsignor beckoned for him to enter and sit down. "Need to talk to you."

Kavanaugh sat down across from the rector. "Something's come up?"

"Unfortunately." He waved the file in the air. "It's Stanley Rother's grades. They are miserable and he can't get a grip on Latin. I don't see how we can allow him to continue."

"I see," Fr. Kavanaugh said slowly. "I must say Stanley is one of the finest students we've ever had. I know he's had a hard time with the textbooks, but it hasn't soured him. He's always kept his dignity. A peaceful man in every way. I think Stanley would make a fine priest."

"But he can't master Latin!" the rector objected.

"I must say there are significant leaders who feel that a priest should be far more proficient in their native tongue than in Latin. Perhaps, we could make an exception and…"

"I'm not one of those modernists!" The rector pounded the table. "A priest must know Latin. For nearly 2,000 years we've used Latin textbooks and I'm not for changing that tradition for one farm boy from Oklahoma!"

Kavanaugh shrugged. "I suppose we have differences of opinion." He raised one eyebrow. "Stanley certainly has done plenty of dirty work *for you*."

"That has nothing to do with it," the rector protested and looked miffed. "Students at St. John's and Assumption Seminary must maintain its standards. I would appreciate your informing Stanley Rother that he will not be coming back."

"You want *me* to tell him?" Kavanagh bristled. "Isn't that the administrator's responsibility?"

"You know him better than I and can be understanding. I think that is the best way. I will write a letter to his bishop and let him know we are releasing Stanley."

"I see," the priest said slowly. "If that's your final answer, I will speak with him."

"Thank you, Father. Now, I must write that letter."

Fr. Kavanagh shook his head and left.

The seminary rector turned back to the window and watched Stanley digging in the dirt. "We'll sure miss him."

***

The news spread quickly. Although confidential, gossip leaked the results and soon virtually every student heard Stanley would not be coming back. Joseph Parsons met him at supper time just before they entered the dining room.

"I'm afraid I've heard bad news," Joseph said.

Stanley only nodded.

"Maybe it's only a rumor."

"They haven't talked to me yet, but I did flunk the first semester. I'm afraid what's you have heard is true. I don't think I'll be coming back."

Joseph patted him on the shoulder. "Don't give up, brother. I'm convinced there are alternatives."

"Thank you." Stanley smiled a faint grin but walked away. The situation was too painful.

The seminarians ate together in a dignified style with only a few quiet jokes passed around the tables under the breath. No one said anything to him, but they all knew. As they were finishing, Fr. Kavanaugh stopped and spoke quietly. "Could I see you as soon as the meal is finished. No hurry. I'll be in my office."

Stanley nodded but said nothing. He knew. Everyone knew.

The walk down the hall seemed to take forever. A multitude of thoughts ran through his mind as he trudged along. What would his parents think? His sister already a nun? The rejection felt embarrassing and so disappointing. He turned the corner and found the man who had always been his friend waiting behind his desk.

"Come in, Stan," Fr. Kavanaugh said. "Sit down. Maybe I could pour you a little drink?"

"Thank you, but I already know what this is about. I guess someone leaked the word to the student body. I know I won't be allowed to come back."

The priest nodded quietly. "You are a fine young man and I know there will be many other fields of service. Perhaps, you could complete your initial college work in Oklahoma before you apply again. Would that be possible?"

Stanley shrugged. "I'm not sure. Perhaps I ought to go back to being a farmer. That's something I know about."

"There's nothing wrong with being a farmer, Stan. Honorable indeed, but you must find what you've been called to be. not let this bump in the road stop you from trying."

"I guess the seminary has already written to Bishop Reed that I'll be coming back to Oklahoma?"

"Afraid so. The semester is virtually over. You can leave anytime."

Stanley took a deep breath. "I understand."

"You are an excellent man," the teacher said. "Don't give up yet."

"Yes sir. Thank you." Stanley got up and forced a smile. He closed the office door behind him and started back down the long hall that now seemed longer than ever.

***

Bishop Victor Reed read the letter twice and bit his lip. No good news there. He had liked Stanley Rother from the first time he met him. A good Oklahoma boy from the red dirt country. Too fine a person to be turned out of a seminary. Something had to be done. The bishop knew he must meet Stanley as soon as he returned. A flight back must be arranged, and he should be met at the airport like a dignitary, not a failure. He must do everything possible to sustain this fine young man.

The Bishop pushed the button on his intercom. "Is Sister Clarisa still here?"

"I believe so," the secretary answered.

"Would you please find her. I want her to write a letter for me."

9

Everything was shutting down. The semester had now finished. Stanley spent the day getting his house in order and packing up. Now that the classes were over, other students would be doing the same. He had little left to do. Nothing big, small items, but the putting stuff in boxes took time and there were people he had to speak too, appreciation to teachers who helped. Stanley guessed he might never see any of them again and many had become friends. When he bumped into them, they all wished him the best. The conversations tended to be superficial as no one wanted to touch what lurked painfully just below the surface of his smile.

"Well, Joseph. I know you'll be wrapping up things here and going on to a higher-level seminary. Where to?"

"The bishop is talking about Washington, D.C. Two excellent seminaries there. Either seminary would be fine and of course Josephite Seminary is there. We'll see."

"Bless you," Stan said and shook his hand and hurried away leaving, Joseph Parsons standing there. Without stopping, he continued down the hall toward his room.

"Oh, Stanley!" Someone called behind him. One of the secretaries from the administration offices hurried toward him. He remembered her name had been Martha something or the other. He turned.

"Yes, ma'am?"

"A special delivery letter just came for you. The envelope heading says Bishop Victor Reed."

"Oh! Thank you." He took the letter and sat down on a bench. For a moment, he flinched. Probably more bad news... like don't come back to Oklahoma. He opened the envelope.

The letter wasn't from the bishop, but his old teacher Sister Clarisa.

Dear, dear Stanley,

The Bishop asked me to write. He is covering an airflight for you back to Oklahoma City and looks forward to seeing you. Of course, we know about the bad news, but listen to me carefully, my old 5th grade student. Do not! And I repeat do not let this problem sidetrack you. God has a plan for your life and no seminary is going to stop it.

I want you to remember the Cure of Ars. St. John Vianney struggled with his academic studies and found Latin to be particularly difficult. Yet, he went on to become the patron of all priests. Let the Cure de Arc be your guide.

Stanley, I know this is a major disappointment, but it is not the end of the line.

Only a bump in the road. This is God's business, and you must trust God to lead you through the hard times. Don't worry, the Almighty will carry you forward.

We will all be here waiting to see you.

The Making of a Martyr

God bless you, Stanley. The sun will rise on another day.

Your friend and 5th grade teacher who knows you best.
Sister Clarisa

Stanley stared at the letter. He couldn't believe what he read. They were not angry with him? The letter said they would welcome him home. For a moment, he wanted to cry. Everything seemed to be too good to be true. The bishop would be there to welcome him back? Amazing. He leaped to his feet to finish packing as quickly as possible. Amazing!"

***

The airplane circled over Oklahoma City and prepared to land. Stanley looked down at his hands. So often, the red dirt had been buried under his fingernails. He loved the land and the smell of wheat ripening in the spring. The wind whistling across the prairie as Fall became colder and always tickled his ears. Watching the winter wheat sprout and start to grow through cold winter days marked the passing of the seasons. The clay-colored land was in his blood. As the plane lowered for the runway, he remembered the smell of the golden oil they put in the tractor and the roar of the engine when it came to life. Maybe that was where he belonged after all. The airplane hit the runway and bounced, whirled around and headed for the gate.

For a moment, Stan bit his lip. Maybe no one would be there. That old miserable feeling that he wasn't that important swelled up. Maybe he was just a farmer coming back from an adventure that didn't turn out well. He had to take it all in stride.

The passengers lined up to walk out. He wondered if his old room on the family farm in Okarche was still there for him. Would they let him come back until he figured out what to do next? He started following the passengers out of the airplane.

"Stanley!" His mother Gertrude rushed forward to hug him. His father Franz stood behind her with his hand out. "Welcome home, son," she said.

"Wonderful to see you!" Bishop Victor Reed stood up and rushed over to pat him on the back. "Glad you're here."

Stanley could hardly speak.

"Looking forward to supper with you tonight," the bishop said. "We have so much to talk about."

Stanley could only nod to each of them like a schoolboy lost in the woods coming home for the first time since getting disoriented.

"And here's someone who wants to say hello," the bishop said.

"Sister Clarisa!" Stanley gasped.

"We wanted you to know how proud we are of you," Sister said. "Welcome back for the next part of your journey."

Stanley could only shake his head.

"I'll see you tonight at the Petroleum Club Restaurant," Bishop Reed said. "See you then." He walked away.

"Like I told you," Sister Clarisa said. "The journey has only just begun."

***

At the top of Founders Tower, a circular rotating platform took diners completely around Oklahoma City 360 ^{0} while an elegant meal was served on the finest China with cut crystal glassware. The restaurant graced the city with a touch of refinement and class. The meals at St. John's had not been sparse, but from a different world than this top of the city eating establishment.

Bishop Reed was already waiting when Stanley walked in. "Ah, sit down my boy," he waved him over. "You'll like this place."

"Thank you for meeting with me," Stanley said. "Sure is nice."

"Wouldn't have it any other way."

"I know my failure is a disappointment," Stanley began. "But I …"

"My son, we all have times when we have stumbled," the bishop began. "St. John's was a trial run and helped me see what your needs are. Latin and Logic are not unimportant but there are other areas and qualities that are equally important in making a good priest. I read an excellent report on your character and devotion. We just need to find the right place for you."

Stanley's mouth dropped slightly. "You mean it?"

"Of course. I have already arranged for you to attend a summer session at Conception Seminary. The Benedictine Monks that operate the school have specific instruction to guide you through a special course in Latin. They will help you work through the issues. Don't worry. Those Benedictines are good teachers. Once you've completed their instruction, in the Fall you will attend Mount St. Mary's Seminary in Emmitsburg, Maryland."

Stanley could hardly speak. "I-I d-don't know what to say."

Bishop Reed smiled. "Just part of my job to make sure they treat you right. We believe God has his hand on you, Stan. You have a special work to do. We're going to make sure that you get there."

"I-I thought I was finished."

"Heavens no! You've just started. Don't worry. We are all with you and will make sure you get through seminary. Oh, by the way. Your sister Betty Mae... of course now Sister Marita ... wanted you to know that she has enlisted the class she teaches in Wichita to pray each day for you. Young man, you have an army praying for your success."

Stanley rubbed his face. "I just don't know what to say. I never expected such concern."

"My boy, you have the support of heaven behind you. The hand of God rests on you. Don't worry. The door into your future has only begun to open."

10

Fall 1959

Emmitsburg got its name from William Emmit in 1785. A settlement had been there earlier, but the British restricted colonists' expansion during the French - Indian War. George Bager built a Lutheran Church in the village in 1757, they shared the building with some German Reformed people for a time. However, after the American Revolutionary War, a Roman Catholic missionary, the Rev. Jean Dubois, built a mission church and the seminary. Elizabeth Ann Seton built a school and a hospital on the grounds and was to become the first American Saint. The town was fortified to stop the Confederates invasion in June 1863 which resulted in half the town being burned down. The rumor was a Union sympathizer started "The Great Fire" to prevent the Confederates from raiding the town to take supplies. The actual battle took place twelve miles north in Pennsylvania near a little town named Gettysburg. The world forever remembers that famous struggle.

Far from the flat lands of Oklahoma, Mount St. Mary's College and Seminary sprang up in the tree- covered rolling mountains at the start of the Blue Ridge Mountains with their breath-taking beauty. Surrounded by Colonial style homes, the campus had its own captivating beauty. Stanley had landed in a country of unsurpassed beauty that naturally inspired the best in people. Once more he was starting a new beginning.

Stanley and one of his uncles drove their Ford pickup 1,300 miles from Okarche across Kansas, Missouri, over the Mississippi River on through Kentucky and Pennsylvania, heading ever North. They pulled into a town that looked forever different from the rural villages of Oklahoma. The towering trees had taken on a touch of red and gold that meant Fall wasn't far away. They pulled up in the parking lot of the five-story seminary building.

"Wow!" Stanley said. "Would you look at that structure! What an edifice!"

"Yeah," his uncle said. "Almost never seen nothing like it."

"I don't look much like a seminarian in these traveling clothes, but I guess I might as well go in and see what I need to do to enter the seminary."

Stanley started across the campus. A few students were coming and going from the building. When he walked in, he immediately knew this impressive seminary had been there a long time. The atmosphere seemed to reflect the many years that had passed in those hallowed halls.

"I'm looking for the rector Monsignor George Mulcahy," he asked a young man walking by in a long black cassock.

The student looked over his shoulder. "The office is two doors down."

"Thank you." Stanley kept walking but noticed other men similarly dressed in black cassocks. They smiled and nodded pleasantly.

When he walked in, the secretary looked at him and glanced at his short-sleeved shirt. "You have an appointment?"

"No, I just arrived on campus, but I believe the rector is expecting me. My name is Stanley Rother."

She pursed her lips and frowned. "I'll see." The lady pushed the buttons on her intercom. "A Mister Stanley Rother says you are expecting him." The machine clicked off.

The inner door flew open. A smiling man burst out. "Stanley, my man! So good to see you! Glad you're here."

The secretary's eyes widened, and she shook her head.

"Come in, come in. You must have just arrived."

"Only minutes ago, Father."

"I've been expecting you. Bishop Reed called and sent me a letter. He highly recommended you and said we should take good care of you. Come in and sit down." He shut the door behind them. "I'm going to be your mentor."

***

After his uncle left, Stanley began unpacking and hanging his few clothes in the closet. His long black cassock would be worn every day, so it needed to hang straight to make sure all the wrinkles fell out. A clerical collar and a black shirt were hung next to the cassock. The small room would work fine. Many, many seminarians had lived in this same space and gone on to important ministries. On their knees they had prayed by the bed or on the kneeler. In this simple room, they had wrestled with their personal issues and their academic struggles. Hopefully some of that sanctity had permeated the walls, the desk, the chair and would impart tenacity to him in his striving to succeed. He hung the last shirt in the closet and closed the door.

Stanley sat down on the edge of the bed; he thought about how different this world was. Looking out the window at the massive trees reaching up to the sky from the rolling hills, he remembered the flat lands of Oklahoma. Those red-colored fields didn't have the beauty of what would become the Blue Ridge mountains, but they had imparted their own gifts to him.

Life in Oklahoma had been peaceful, predictable, stable and that had imbedded in him a sense of stability. His family had surrounded him with a sense of order and an expectation of devotion. He had grown up in that two-story white house knowing he was to start the day with prayer, pray at meals, and pray before going to sleep at night. Prayer was essential. No one had to be special to be considered a good person. What counted was what the Psalmist called "uprightness," honesty, straight forwardness, no deception. The Church had taught him to line up his life with the commandments of God, to seek the blessing of the saints, and of course to pray. He knew these gifts and qualities had come with him to Mount Saint Mary's seminary. Now, if only he could succeed in his studies.

Monsignor Mulcahy certainly appeared to be a more supportive alternative to what he had previously experienced. The rector seemed to have his best interests at heart and wanted him to succeed. He couldn't have expected a more positive introduction. Another hopeful sign.

Stanley stretched out on the bed and closed his eyes. The day had been filled with apprehension and some anxiety. Now he fully realized how anxious he had been to meet the rector, but all had gone so well. Stanley relaxed. "Please help me blessed Virgin Mary, empower me heavenly Father." Drowsiness settled in and he drifted away.

11

Winter 1960

The leaves of Autumn languished beneath the snow. The bright observances of Christmas had given way to the bitter cold of January. Monsignor Mulcahy had many regular visits with Stanley and made frequent inquiries about his progress with his professors. The morning Mass started each day. For an alternative, he played basketball with the other students and sang in the chapel. His fine tenor-voice added to the choir. Life at Mount St. Mary's fit him well. Stanley worked hard through these long cold months.

The rector sat at his desk dialing a familiar number. The phone rang several times.

"Diocesan office," a woman's voice said.

"Monsignor Mulcahy here, I need to speak with Bishop Reed."

"One moment please."

"Bishop Reed speaking."

"Ah, your Excellency. It's Monsignor Mulcahy with another report."

"Well, George. How is our boy doing?"

"You'll be pleased. As we discussed earlier, Stanley finished the first semester quite satisfactorily. At this point in the winter term, he continues to sail along in great shape. I think we've defeated that haunting Spectre of Latin. Has raised his grade point to an 85."

"Excellent. I'm sure his mentor had something to do with his success."

Mulcahy laughed. "Oh, of course! No, the truth is that we've never had anyone who worked harder than Stan. The man is excellent. We've found him to be of the highest character. Your boy is making the grade."

"Just what I expected. I knew we had to get Stanley in the right situation. You've provided that setting for him. We are grateful."

"We have found his personal devotion to be of the highest order. Your Excellency, you know I am a very practical man. Oh yes, I get accused of being high handed every now and then, but I understand what's needed to develop a priest. The academics have a place, but I'm looking for good judgment, stability, integrity, and true faith. I find all of those qualities in your man. I believe Stanley will make a fine priest."

"Excellent," Bishop Reed said. "Thank you so much for the call. His parents will be pleased.

***

The cold winter months did not inhibit Stanley's long walks down the trails around Mount St. Mary's. He continued in the seminary's sports programs and found his way into helping with practical needs. He even established a book bindery for the school. His face became familiar and welcomed across the campus. Still, Stanley particularly spent time in the grotto at the Marian Shrine dedicated to Our Lady of Lourdes.

Surrounded by tall trees and an abundance of flowers in the summertime, the shrine had been constructed out of rocks cemented together to emulate the grotto at Lourdes, France. A statue of Mary was placed up in the rocks above the small cave. Inside was a large rack of candles beneath a crucifix. A simple rock altar stood in front. During warmer weather potted plants were placed in front of the altar. Regardless of the weather, Stanley made a regular pilgrimage to the grotto.

Monsignor Hugh Phillips kept the library and was the director of the grotto. He often observed Stan coming down to the cave and kneeling on a cold February afternoon. He walked in just as Stanley was leaving. The monsignor stopped.

"Stanley, I have observed that you made frequent visits to our shrine. You have a devotion to the Blessed Mother Mary."

Stanley shrugged. "I need all the help I can get, I guess." He chuckled.

Monsignor Philips nodded. "Good point. However, I believe there is more in your visits than seeking a blessing. I'm wondering if you don't have a special relationship with our Lady."

"I hope so. I am always blessed when I come here. So, I come often." Stanley smiled, nodded, and started walking away.

Monsignor Phillips watched him walk back down the path. "He has a tender devotion to the Blessed Mother," he said to himself. "Her love will certainly pull him through."

***

The rector walked into the seminary snack bar area and poured himself a cup of coffee. He sat down at one of the small tables and took a sip. Monsignor Hugh Phillips strolled in and stopped at the table.

"How's the library running these days," Fr. Mulcahy asked. "The men keeping you busy?"

Monsignor Phillips laughed. "Are you kidding. I thought libraries were supposed to be quiet. Actually, our students are making good use of the stacks. Got no complaints.

Other teachers walked in for a break and sat around the room. They always gave a polite nod to the rector.

"Our school year is beginning to wind down," Mulcahy said. "Spring's about to break out. Hope all that cold weather is gone. I'm sure that cuts down on visits to the grotto."

"Weather does have an effect. About the only person that nothing bothers is Stanley Rother. I suppose a farm boy is used to the cold weather."

The rector took another sip. "I've observed that Stanley is there nearly every day. No question but that he is quite attentive."

"Um-hmm. Stanley is an interesting guy to talk to. He never promotes himself and is always thoughtful. There's a simplicity about him that is anything but simple. Stanley is one of the most committed people around here. If anything, he is a man of prayer. He seems to have a special relationship with God."

"His bishop is certainly interested in his progress. I hear from Bishop Reed consistently. He certainly wants Stanley to succeed."

Monsignor Phillips nodded. "I have a suggestion. I'd like to see how Stanley does with some practical ministry. We received a call from the tuberculosis sanatorium for someone to help a man named Hall. Why don't we send Stanley over there to talk with this guy?

Apparently, he's struggling and maybe getting desperate. I'd be interested in how Stanley does in talking with this man. After all, a hurting patient would be a challenge."

"Interesting idea. Sure. I'll call Stanley in and talk with him. Be an interesting experience."

Hugh Phillips took another sip of coffee. "Let me know what happens."

12

Wearing his black suit and a clerical collar, Stanley walked into the sanatorium. An antiseptic smell permeated the waiting room. Only three other people sat in the reception area waiting to visit someone. A lonely aura hung over the hospital. Stanley nodded pleasantly to them and walked to the desk. A receptionist looked up.

"I'm here to see a Mr. David Hall."

The woman flipped through the pages on a clip board in front of her. "Oh yes. Mr. Hall is in room 134. You can go on back."

Stanley knew the tuberculosis sanatorium was not exactly the safest place to visit, but that was beside the point. A priest walked in where other visitors feared to go. He started down the long hall and then turned the corner at the other end. A doctor walked by holding a chart but didn't look up. Room 134 was just ahead.

Stanley knocked. A feeble voice invited him to enter.

"Mr. Hall? David Hall?"

The man lying in a hospital bed under a white cotton blanket raised up. "Oh, you came. Thank goodness that you answered my call."

David Hall looked like he must at least be in his seventies, but his condition would have aged him, so it wasn't possible to tell. His drawn face and pale complexion conveyed the seriousness of his condition. What was left of his hair had thinned and looked like it hadn't been combed in days. He stretched out a skinny arm. "Please come closer."

Stanley walked in and stood by the bed. "We received your call at Mount St. Mary's. What can I do for you?"

David Hall rubbed his forehead. "They tell me that I might not make it. I ain't doing any good. My lungs are shot, and my heart's all worn out. It is hard to breathe. Every day is a struggle. I'm afraid I'm on my last leg."

"I understand," Stanley said. "Why did you call a seminarian?"

David Hall shook his head. "I never gave my religious life any thought. Never went to church. Broke my mother's heart. I wasn't a bad man … but wasn't all that good either. Now that I'm at the end of the road I don't know what to do. Can you help me?"

"I can't help you, but the Lord can," Stanley began. "David, all those years He was waiting for you. Even now His hand is extended to you."

"How can a shriveled up old fool like me believe that?"

Stanley picked up a Bible that someone had place on the windowsill. "Ever hear of the Prodigal Son?"

David Hall shook his head. "Nope."

"The Gospel of Luke tells the story of a man who took his inheritance from his father, went off to a foreign land and squandered it in foolish living. Starving and broken he came home feeling worthy only to live with the animals. When he returned, his father ran out to greet him, put a ring on his finger, and welcomed him like a returning prince. Jesus told that parable for people like you, Mr. Hall. That's the way your heavenly Father is waiting for you to come to him."

The old man stared. "How can that be?"

"Because that's the way God loves us. Regardless of your past, the Lord Jesus is still beckoning for you to come to him. He never changes."

David Hall fell back on his pillow and took a deep breath. "I've made so many mistakes," he uttered under his breath. "I-I don't know."

"The story of Jesus on the Cross is about his dying for those mistakes, Mr. Hall. We call those errors sins. Jesus died for your sins."

He put both hands over his face and rubbed his cheeks. "I didn't expect you to be so direct."

"You don't have the time for anything other than my getting to the point."

David Hall sighed. "I've got to think about all of this. Got to let it settle."

Stanley handed him the Bible. That story is in the 15th chapter of Luke. Read the entire gospel for yourself. Think on it. I believe the account will give you direction."

The old man reached over and took Stanley's hand. "Give me a little time. Will you come back tomorrow?"

"Sure. I'll be here at about the same time."

"Thank you. Thank you so much. I'll be waiting."

***

The next afternoon, Stanley returned to the sanatorium, carrying a Missal. The same receptionist immediately recognized and welcomed him. "Glad to see you. Mr. Hall has been talking about your visit all day. You made quite an impression on him.

Stanley smiled. "Nice to hear. I guess he's waiting to talk with me."

"You bet. He's been telling the nurses that you were coming. Go on back."

Once more Stanley started down the spotless hall looking for room 134. The irritating antiseptic smell couldn't be avoided. He had barely knocked on the room when David Hall called him in. The feeble voice sounded like it had more vitality than before. Stanley walked in.

"Ah, Father! You've come back!" David Hall exclaimed.

"Actually, I'm only a seminarian."

"Whatever. I don't know about these matters. I just want you to talk to me some more. I read the story in Luke's gospel. Read it five times. Just couldn't believe my eyes."

"You doubted the story?"

"Oh no! It all just seemed to be too good to be true."

Stanley chuckled. "I understand. I think we all have times where we feel like the Prodigal did. Hard to believe that we are accepted by God while we are in that state of mind."

Hall shook his head. "Oh, yes. But you really believe this is all true?"

"I'd stake my life on it."

The old man rubbed his eyes. "Father, I don't have much time left. The T.B. is bad enough, but my heart's just worn out. I'm almost too weak to get out of bed. I know the clock is running down."

Stanley said nothing. Total quietness settled over the room.

Finally, David Hall said, "What do I need to do to get right with God?"

"Do you believe in Jesus? Believe in him as your savior?"

"Been thinking about that question all night. Yes, yes I do. I don't know as much as I should know, but I do believe in him. I don't see how he can believe in me."

"In all of our churches you will find a crucifix. The dramatic picture or sculpture of the crucified Jesus is a depiction of the fact he died for you while you paid him no attention. Jesus died not only for your sin but also for your doubts. All he asks is for you to come home."

The old man began to weep. "I *do* believe," he could barely utter. I *do believe*."

"Then you need to be baptized and ask the Holy Spirit to fully guide your life."

"I want that," David Hall muttered. "I want all of it."

"Then we need to baptize you and ask Jesus to cleanse you of all sins."

"Can we do that today?" David Hall pushed himself up on his elbows. Would you do that right now?"

"Do you have water here and ..."

"There's a hydrant over there. You can say a prayer or whatever over that water. I want to be baptized this afternoon."

Stanley studied his drawn face. All color was gone. The thinning strands of white were tangled and some of his hair stood on end. Stanley felt he couldn't let this moment pass. He opened the Missal and placed the leather-bound prayer book on the nightstand.

Picking up a small cup, he opened the faucet and poured in water. David Hall settled back on his pillow and closed his eyes. Stanley stood over him.

"Do you reject Satan and all his works?"

"Yes, I must certainly do," David Hall said.

"Do you reject sin and all of its glamor."

"Definitely."

"Do you reject Satan, the father of sin, and prince of darkness?"

"I do." Tears began rolling down Hall's face. "I do."

Stanley began leading him through the Apostles Creed, asking him to affirm his faith line by line. Though halting, Hall's answers were certain. "I do accept and believe in Jesus Christ," he mumbled again and folded his hands in front of his chest.

Holding the cup of water above his head. Stanley said, "I baptize you in the name of the Father." He poured some of the water on him. "And in the name of the Son." Again, he poured water on him. "And in the name of the Holy Spirit." He poured the rest on him.

"Thank you," David whispered.

"I won't be here next year anyway," David said.

"Let's say the Lord's Prayer together." Stanley had barely begun when he realized David could only fumble through the words, but they kept praying.

David smiled, nodded, and closed his eyes. "Thank you, thank you ever so much."

Stanley closed the Missal and quietly slipped away.

***

As soon as he returned to Mount St. Mary's, he went into the rector's office. "Could I see Monsignor Mulcahy?"

The secretary looked up. This time she smiled. "Certainly." She pushed the intercom button. "Stanley here to see you." She pointed to the door for him to go on in.

"My boy!" The rector stood up. "How's it going?"

"Fine, sir. I just baptized David Hall over at the sanitorium."

"Really!" Mulcahy's eyes opened wide in surprise.

"The poor man doesn't have much time left and asked me to do so right then."

"You ever baptized anyone before?"

Stanley shook his head. "No. My first time. Of course, I watched baptisms at home."

Mulcahy rubbed his chin. "You never cease to surprise me, Stan. Oh, yes. That was the right thing to do. One can never tell about these matters. Time can be of the essence. Well, excellent work, Stan. You'll need to check on him tomorrow." He sat down behind his desk. "I'll make a note of this for your file. Yes, good work indeed."

Stanley nodded and left the office. The rector sat there smiling, watching him walk away.

***

The next afternoon, Stanley returned to the sanatorium. The time an older lady sat at the receptionist desk. She obviously didn't recognize him. "Can I help you?"

"I'm here to see David Hall."

"Umm, let me see. Something came in this morning. Oh, yes, here is the notification. David Hall passed away last night."

Wise

13

May 1963

Spring inspired the trees on the Blue Ridge Mountains to explode with a fresh covering of leaves. Flowers sprung up around the seminary building. The air spelled sweet and pure. The semester was over, and the classes finished. Monsignor George Mulcahy met Stanley as he was preparing to load his things in his truck for the long journey home. Standing on the steps of the entry to Mount St. Mary, both men smiled at each other. Four years had passed rapidly bringing the two men into an even closer relationship.

"My boy, you made it. Here you are a deacon ready to be ordained a priest in just a few days. Seems like only yesterday when you came walking into my office in jeans looking like a farm boy straight out of the fields. And now you are about to be ordained a priest. What can I say?"

"Monsignor, you've been extremely kind to me. Kept me on track and doing my studies. I can never thank you enough for your oversight and help."

"It was nothing. You're the one who did the hard work. I was on the phone yesterday talking with your Bishop, thanking him for sending you here. He, too, is very proud of your success. Sorry that I can't be there for your ordination. I know your family is proud."

Stanley smiled. "Mom and Pop will certainly be there with big smiles. I know they would thank you too."

"Give them my best," the rector said. "Hope to see them some day. Your little sister now become Sister Marita is equally proud of your accomplishments. Two religious in one family! You must have a devout family."

"Indeed."

"Well, the best to you, Stan. God bless you, my boy." The rector bit his lip, turned quickly and walked back up the steps. "Write me from time to time," he said over his shoulder.

Stanley waved, picked up his final bag and threw it in the back of his pickup. He started down the long road back to Oklahoma City. In four days, he would walk down the center aisle in the Cathedral of Our Lady of Perpetual Help in Oklahoma City. Bishop Reed would be there waiting to ordain him. Stanley Rother was about to become Father Rother.

***

The Indian settlement territory had been opened by the land run in 1889 when a gun was fired and men on horseback and families in wagons raced across the flat plains to claim land. Overnight Oklahoma City and Guthrie were born and a new state was about to come into being. The first Bishop of Oklahoma Theophile Meerschaert founded Our Lady of Perpetual Help Parish in 1919. Monsignor Albert Monnot was appointed Pastor, January 16, 1919, to a parish covering eighty square miles that would serve the northwest expansion of Oklahoma City. On May 15 and 16 of 1919, twelve men worked for two days to build a temporary wooden church building on property recently purchased by the Parish. Masses had been celebrated in the school for four years and then construction began on the Church July 3, 1923. The last brick was laid in February of 1924, completing the construction of the new church. The magnificent brick building with its large central stained-glass window shining down on the edifice provided the setting for ordinations.

A beautiful church became the cathedral in1930 with blue arches and stone columns supporting the long sanctuary, as cathedral Our Lady's was the principal church of the Oklahoma Dioceses. Stained glass windows and hanging lights would reflect on the candidates as they lay prostrate on the floor. Along with eleven other candidates, Deacon Stanley Rother prepared to enter the Cathedral and stand before Bishop Reed for this life- changing moment when he would become a priest.

On the morning of May 25, 1963, the rite of Ordination began. The organ played a prelude that seemed to impart a holy aura over the gathering congregation. The bishop in his miter, and chasable would lay his hands on Stanley's head. Through the ancient rite, he would become a priest of Jesus Christ. Stanley would surrender his life to the purposes of the Holy Spirit and his future would forever be in the hands of the heavenly Father. Stanley knew his destiny was about to begin.

The processional hymn signaled the clergy and ordinands entering down the central aisle had begun. With the candidates dressed in white albs, the men walked together with the packed crowd on both sides of the aisles watching with anticipation.

Although he couldn't see them, Stanley knew his parents were there somewhere. Brothers Tom and Jim would be standing on tiptoe to see. Of course, Betty Mae now Sister Marita would be observing every second of the liturgy and praying for him. He could never forget how she had marshalled her students to pray for him. No telling how many had interceded for his success. A sea of faces flashed before his eyes as he walked slowly down the aisle. Teachers who had helped and inspired him as well as a few who cared only for the subject matter emerged in his memory. Classmates who would forever be his friends. How could he ever forget Bishop Victor Reed? He still found it hard to realize that the bishop had gone out of his way to find a place in the right seminary. Of course, the face of Sister Clarissa Tenbrink would always be in his reflections. From the fifth grade forward, she had seen a promise in him that he knew nothing about. Her messages to him at critical times when he doubted himself had carried him through dark days. Somewhere in the crowd, Sister Clarissa would be smiling.

As the ordinands filed into their pew, the Holy Spirit seemed to whisper in his mind. This day was supremely important, but another day was coming of even greater significance. Whatever was ahead, today Stanley was ready to lay his life on the line.

The organ stopped playing. Bishop Reed stretched out his arms. "Beloved in the Lord, we have come to ordain a minister of Word and sacrament in Christ's holy church. Christ alone is the source of all Christian ministry, through the ages calling men and women to serve ..."

Stanley took a deep breath and closed his eyes. It was happening.

The Making of a Martyr

PART TWO

"For my own sake, I am a Christian. For the sake of others, I am a priest."
St. Augustine
--Father Stanley Rother

14

Who could have guessed that the Sixties would become a decade of turmoil and chaos? Civil rights demonstrations sent thousands into the streets, marching for justice while the war in Vietnam became a boiling caldron of discontent. Families split over these issues. President John Kennedy was assassinated followed by the killing of his brother Robert. Martin Luther King Jr. was murdered in Memphis. Pope John XXIII died during the Vatican II sessions. Three weeks later, Paul VI was elected, and the Second Vatican Council continued. Change was everywhere.

The new priest found himself swept up in the sweeping winds of change. Appointed to a quiet parish in Durant, Oklahoma, Fr. Rother went about the business of caring for the parish. St. William's Church had the usual needs of every parish.

The door on the Confessional slid open. "Bless me Father, for I have sinned," the women's voice said.

"What is your sin?" Father Rother asked.

The woman rolled off a meaningless and innocuous recitation that hardly had any meaning. He listened silently as she rattled on. Her words hardly revealed the depth of her true need.

Fr. Rother scratched his head. "Nothing more?"

"I guess not."

He suggested her penance and slid the small door shut. Life in the small town surely had more depth than this.

Each day in Durant rolled along predictably and peacefully. Of course, there were moments when the national protests spilled over, but for the most part the confrontations were far away. While going about the church's business, Fr. Stanley found a meaningful relationship with members of an American Indian tribe. He seemed to have a natural attraction to these people. The husband worked for the Highway Patrol and the wife was the mother to three children. The Red Bird family found Fr. Stanley to be a close friend. Their daughter Mary attended the local college. In turn, he particularly enjoyed them. Fr. Rother seemed to have a knack for working with people of this background. During this time, he met Carol Sowatikee, a mixture of Caddo, Cheyenne, and Cherokee tribes.

Wearing casual clothes, Fr. Stan was walking across the Southeastern State College campus when he saw Mary Red Bird and another Indian girl coming toward him. "Hello ladies. How are you?"

Mary smiled. "Doing good. This is my friend Carol Sowatikee."

"Carol! Nice to meet you."

She smiled. Mary whispered. "He's a priest."

Carol eyes him suspiciously. "How come you don't have on your priest suit?"

Fr. Stanley laughed. "I'm taking a break."

Carol Sowatikee glared. "Is it true that you Catholics worship idols?"

"Carol, you come right to the point. I like that. No, Catholics only worship the Lord God and His Son, Jesus Christ. We have the utmost respect for the Virgin Mary as well as saintly people from the past, but we don't worship them."

"Surprising," Carol said. "You look me straight in the eyes when you talk. I respect that. I guess I don't know anything really about your church except hearsay."

"You ought to visit on Sunday," Mary Red Bird said. "You might be surprised at what you would find."

"St. Williams isn't far from the campus," Fr. Stanley said. "Come over at 10:00."

Carol Sowatikee smiled and shrugged.

***

The spring season of Pentecost always brought vestments trimmed in red. The chasable at St. Williams had an especially striking color. When Fr. Stanley came down the aisle in a red chasuble, Carol Sowatikee took note. Red was her favorite color.

"In the name of the Father, Son, and Holy Spirit," Fr. Rother made the sign of the cross and began the liturgy.

Carol stared. This was not at all what she expected. The church was so quiet and respectful. The one her grandmother took her too was loud and spontaneous in a folksy way. As the liturgy moved along, she found herself surprisingly drawn to what was unfolding. The music was different but inviting and moving. Mary could tell that this Fr. Rother was a kind and genuine man. Perhaps he would be open to some of her unanswered questions. Just maybe, she could talk to him.

The Mass ended. The priest processed out while the congregation sang the last hymn. People began moving to the back door. Carol fell in with them.

"Carol!" Fr. Stanley warmly shook her hand. "So glad you came."

She glanced away, feeling a little embarrassed that he recognized her.

"Certainly hope you'll come back."

"I know that you are a very busy man," Carol said haltingly. "But I would like to talk with you privately."

"I'd be delighted. Any time you're ready, I'll be here. In fact, I'd look forward to talking to you."

"Thank you," Carol kept looking down. "I'll call you."

* * *

During the summer months, Carol Sowatikee came by the priest's office often. Fr. Stanley answered her many questions and helped her find new insight into the Christian faith. Her family had developed some strange beliefs and fears about such things as poltergeists and evil spirits. The priest was able to help Carol set aside her superstitions and anxieties. She knew she had found a true friend as well as spiritual guide.

During the first week in September, Carol came in with a grim face. She sat down and stared at the floor.

For a moment, he studied her downcast look. "What's wrong?" Fr. Stanley asked.

"I've told you about my problems with my boyfriend. It's all become much more serious."

Fr. Stanley settled back in his desk chair and watched her eyes. "What's happened?"

Carol burst into tears. For several moments, she sobbed and then finally caught her breath. "I'm pregnant. I've just come from the doctor. He told me that I could go to Catholic Charities in Oklahoma City for help." Carol began weeping again. "My boyfriend has disappeared, and I have no other alternative."

"I know you are terrified but let me reassure you that this problem does not alter God's plan for your life. Your heavenly Father continues His oversight of your life. Catholic Charities will place you with a family that will care for you during this time. You will find consolation that will sustain you."

"Do you really think so?"

"Carol, I know what it's like to think you've come to the end of your hope, and everything is hopeless. I've been there, but I also know in the midst of despair, the Holy Spirit is still working, and you will come out the other side victorious."

Carol looked at him for a long time. Finally, she said, "You are the most amazing man I have ever met."

15

The summer winds kept blowing dust against the door of Aunt Lou's Café. People in Durant started drifting in around 11:00. The home-made pies and meatloaf attracted a continual stream of customers. Fr. Rother ate there often. An old friend had dropped in to see him. Fr. Ramon Carlin was well known across the Oklahoma Diocese. His white Stetson hat had earned him the nickname "Tex" when in fact he was a graduate of the esteemed Catholic University of Louvain in Belgium. A man of strong opinions, Fr. Tex could make you happy one minute and angry the next.

The two men strolled in an sat in a back booth.

"Say," Fr. Ramon said, "Whatever became of that little Indian girl you were helping? Believe the name was Carol something-or-the-other. I heard about her problem at Catholic Charities. I discovered you had worked with her."

"Carol endured her struggle well," Fr. Stanley answered. "She got on her way and the last that I heard was doing well in Tulsa."

"Good. Good. Always glad to hear of a redemption." He picked up a menu. "What's good here?"

"About anything you order. They make a good bowl of Chili."

"Believe I'll take the chef salad. Good for us fat boys," he joked.

"Tex, I know you well enough to know that you didn't just happen to drive through Durant for your health. You've always got something on your mind."

Fr. Ramon laughed. "My, my, my reputation must be spreading. I did believe in the Second Vatican Council decisions for liturgical change. You gotta' admit that our side won the day."

Fr. Stanley laughed. "And you came all the way out here to make sure we are observant."

"Not exactly. You probably know that several years ago Pope John XIII called for more interest be given to the people of Central America. Bishop Reed picked up that challenge and gave particular concern to a parish in Santiago Atitlan in Guatemala. A nice number of people responded and went down there to help."

"I don't really know anything about that area."

"The Indians are descendants of the Mayans. Bishop Reed has already sent two priests and two lay people down there to help them. They've had a real struggle. I went down there myself. The parish is on the edge of a magnificent blue lake, Lake Atitlan. Fascinating place. The Santiago Apostol parish was founded by the Franciscans in 1536. Built the most interesting church and some surrounding structures. Of course, in 1870, the Guatemalan government ran the Spanish out. The result has been that for the last 100 years they haven't had a resident priest. Those poor people have struggled spiritually and physically ever since."

Fr. Stanley leaned forward. "Most, most interesting. Of course, I learned something of the work of the Franciscans I was in the seminary in San Antonio. I've always been fascinated by their accomplishments. They established so much."

Fr. Tex grinned as if he was hearing what he had hoped for. "Yes, Stan, my man. You do appear to have an inclination for working with Indian people. You apparently have a disposition for missionary work. "

Fr. Stanley shrugged. "I grew up on a farm. Always enjoyed farming. I guess I have a natural inclination for people who have lived so close to nature. I'm really just a boy from the red dirt soil of Oklahoma."

"Exactly!" Tex pointed across the table with his index finger. "You are a natural for the Santiago Apostol parish."

"What?"

"I'm looking for volunteers to go down to Lake Atitlan. You're exactly the right man to be a missionary."

Stanley stiffened. "Me?"

"Why not? The bishop would be glad to appoint you to our missionary team to Guatemala. He has a particular interest in this parish of the Apostle St. James. I know he'd be highly pleased to send you."

"I never thought of myself in that capacity."

"You're too modest, Stan. Your early years in farming prepared you for the tasks in a mission station. And who cares more about Indian people than you? I believe Christ is calling you to this work."

"You don't stop putting the pressure on, do you?" Stanley leaned back and blinked several times. "This is quite a surprise."

"That's why I came today. I want to invite you to join me and come down to the Santiago Apostol parish. The country is magnificent. Towering volcanoes surround the most magnificent lake you've ever seen. Beautiful scenery. It's a completely different world. You'd love it."

For several moments, Fr. Stanley said nothing. Finally, he said, "I'll have to think about the idea, well, pray about it." Once more he became silent. "Quite a thought."

***

Two days had passed since Fr. Ramon Carlin's visit when the church office phone rang. Fr. Stanley immediately picked it up. "St. William Church parish."

"Ah, my boy, good to hear your voice."

"Bishop Reed?"

"Indeed. How are things going in the neighborhood?"

Stanley laughed. "Well, Durant is somewhat of a small town. Don't get a lot of excitement here. I just chug along."

"Oh, I get good reports on your work. I wanted to talk with you about a new appointment."

"Really? Another parish in Oklahoma?"

"Actually, a bit further South. Like in Guatemala."

After a long pause, Fr. Stanley said. "I just had a visit from Fr. Raman Carlin. Has he been talking to you?"

Bishop Reed chuckled. "He was just here. Your name did come up."

"Tex seems intent on me going down to the Santiago Apostol parish. Is that what we are talking about?"

"Stan, you are exactly what we need down there. Your background makes you an excellent missionary candidate. The people of this parish are the 'have nots' of the world. They struggle with many things, but developing good nutrition is certainly part of my concern. What you grew up with on the farm will be vital for them. They need you to teach them to grow better crops as well as meet their spiritual needs. I'd like to send you. Now, if you object, I won't, but that's my desire."

"Bishop, you know I'll go wherever you send me. How well I know that you always have my best interest at heart. If that's what you want, I'll say yes."

"Excellent. I believe you'll love the people and I know they'll love you. I believe you'll find that Jesus Christ is hidden in their need, waiting for you to come and help. You will be able to assist them on every level. I think this settles the matter."

"When will I leave?"

"How about in around two days or so?"

***

Stanley stood outside the rectory looking at his red-and-white Ford Bronco. Driving 2,000 miles down to Lake Atitlan and this far away parish would certainly be a challenging way to begin this new ministry. Could the Ford pickup make it? Yeah, he thought. Maybe better than me. He had just changed the oil and made sure the truck was lubricated.

"Hello, Father."

He turned around to find Mary Red Bird standing behind him. "Mary! What a delightful surprise."

For a moment, she looked sadly at him. "Is it true you are leaving us?"

"I'm afraid so. The bishop has asked me to be a missionary to Guatemala. I'll be leaving shortly."

"My mother and father think of you as part of our family. You have meant so much to us. Needless to say, you also helped Carol Sowatikee turn a tragedy into a new beginning. All of us don't want you to go."

Stanley wiped his greasy hands on a rag. "Mary, I will miss all of you so very much. I'm afraid God is calling me to go to these struggling Indians and help them survive both here and for eternity. The bishop asked me to go and that settled the matter. Yes, I'll miss all of you."

Mary nodded her head solemnly. "I understand." She walked over and kissed him on the cheek. "Thank you, Fr. Stanley. Thank you for all you've done for us." She turned and walked away.

Stanley watched her disappear down the block. Leaving would not be easy.

16

Fall 1968

The hot winds of August had faded, and the temperature began to drop. Stanley had a mechanic take a second look at the red-and-white Ford Bronco. After all, a 2,000-mile trip was no small strain, and he couldn't afford to have some unexpected motor problem leave him stranded in the middle of Mexico. He had already received word that Fr. Tom Stafford would be traveling with him. Stafford had been among the first to go to Guatemala when the call to send missionaries first came in. He would know the way and understand the twists and turns in the road. Fr. Stafford had arrived the night before and was ready to go south.

"We're hauling that 1,000-pound rock mover behind your truck?" Stafford asked.

"It's heavy but very mobile," Fr. Stanley said. "I don't foresee any problems."

"We've quite a journey ahead of us. Think we can drive night and day by exchanging drivers shifts?"

"I don't see why not," Stanley said. "With such a distance, I'd like to keep after it."

"I agree," Stafford said. "I'm ready to roll when you are."

"Get in and I'll turn around. We'll be on our way."

The Ford truck roared to life. Stanley started moving slowly as he turned to head out of the driveway. Suddenly he stopped. The entire Red Bird family were standing on the edge of the rectory's property waving. Stanley slowed to a stop.

"We came to say goodbye," Jack Red Bird said. "My wife baked you some sweet rolls to take with you. Mary wanted to give you this salami to eat with it. We will miss you."

Mary Red Bird handed him a paper sack through the window. "Please be careful."

"Bless you all." The two priests waved. "God's peace be with you."

Fr. Stanley slowly pulled away, waving out the truck window. In the rear-view mirror, he could see the Red Bird family waving long after they had gone down the street. The highway out of Durant turned toward Lake Texoma and then south. It was a long way to the ancient parish.

***

The western highlands of Guatemala were filled with an abundance of foliage, huge trees, and brilliant-colored flowers. However, the further they traveled, the rougher the road became. It felt almost like civilization had been left behind. The rock picker bounced behind the truck as they swerved to avoid potholes sprinkled across the road like explosives in a mine field.

"How long we been traveling?" Fr. Tom asked.

"I calculate about 33 continuous hours. We've done well."

"You'll find the last lap to be hardest and slowest," Stafford said. "The road gets worse, and the forest becomes even more dense. Ever seen anything like this gorgeous country?"

"Never. Breathtaking." Stanley pulled out the map and studied it for a moment. "I'd guess we must be within ten to twenty miles of our destination."

"You'll see that the village of San Lucas Toliman and Santiago Atitlan are the hardest to reach, but we're not far away. The road gets much worse, so we'll have to go slow."

The truck began bouncing harder as the chuck holes got deeper and more frequent. They could see the rock picker popping up and down like a rubber ball.

"Wow!" Fr. Stanley said. "Worse than I expected!"

Fr. Tom kept swerving back and forth, trying to miss the big bumps. Stanley bounced up and down in his seat. Suddenly, a huge hole appeared in front of them. Stafford hit the brakes, but it was too late. The truck took a dip and then convulsed straight up in the air. A ripping sound of metal tearing filled their ears. He came to a stop.

"I'm afraid we just lost the muffler," Stafford said.

"I'll take a look."

After a few moments, Stanley crawled out from underneath the truck. "I think we can kiss the muffler goodbye. Completely tore off. I hope the local citizens in Santiago Atitlan don't mind us driving in sounding like a volcano."

Tom laughed. "They've got no choice."

During the last few miles into the village the roads didn't improve. Consequently, Stafford drove the truck at a crawl.

Eventually Lake Atitlan came into sight. Stanley stuck his head out the window for a better view.

"Would you look at that? That lake is absolutely gorgeous."

"Yes, the most beautiful lake I ever saw."

When they made the final turn into the village, people came out of their houses and waved. Some gawked, while others were excited. The simple, narrow street wound through several blocks until it came to the zocalo, the central plaza. On one side stood the colonial church the Spanish had built so long ago. A few chickens ran here and there. Dogs barked. They came to a stop and Stanley got out.

He knew the Indians were small in stature, but he had no idea how short until he realized he was head and shoulders taller than everyone. His five- foot- ten-inch stature towered over virtually everybody. Men wore cowboy hats and the women had woven serapes with simple striped designs. Some women had heavy, woven scarfs pulled over their heads. With black hair and dark skin, some of the men carried heavy loads on their backs while the women walking beside them balanced vases and bundles on their heads.

People began coming out of every corner and alley. Bright colors flashed in the afternoon sunlight. The people quickly gathered around Fr. Rother's truck as if Christmas had come early and he was Santa Claus. He kept smiling and waving, while trying to digest how much taller he was than everyone else. The Indians kept staring at him almost in amazement at his height.

"You have arrived in MICATOKLA," Fr. Stafford said. "That's the name that the first Oklahomans who came down here gave this place. It stands for Mission Catholica de Oklahoma. That's what the lay people liked to call the town. The villagers were thrilled to death that we had come. I think they may find you even more fascinating since you look like a giant to them."

Stanley waved at the people one more time and then turned toward the Colonial Church. "Think I ought to see where I am going to be celebrating. Why don't you park the truck while I'm inside?"

"Sure." Stafford climbed back inside the Bronco and drove off.

Stanley walked up the steps and opened the large wooden front door. To his surprise, the church was much larger than he expected. Looked like the whole village could get in. Hand woven tapestries hung from the walls. He walked down the center aisle toward the altar. When Stanley got to the front, he genuflected and slid into one of the wooden benches.

"How many people sat here through the centuries?" he said to himself. "Through suffering, tragedy, death, the people have come to this sanctuary for solace. The walls must resonate with their countless prayers."

For a long time, he sat silently, trying to absorb the sanctity of this holy sanctuary where so much had happened through four centuries. These good people had endured so much through the turbulent times in the past. Their endurance had taught them to believe. Now, if only he could earn that same trust.

17

1973

The past three years had passed like a blur. The Tz'utuijil people had generously accepted him and surrounded the priest with affection. He had learned they were the fifth largest tribe of the 21 Mayan groups that made Guatemala their home. The Indians seem to have a natural affection and admiration for him because he was their priest who had come down from that far away country to the North. The passing of time meant little in this remote part of the world, and that fit his farming instinct for waiting for crops to come up in their own season.

The natives had learned that the priest's full name was Stanley Francis Rother, but they couldn't say the name "Stanley" in their language, so he quickly became Padre Francisco or Padre Aplas most of the time. He liked the title and often smiled when they said it.

The rectory dining hall had become the gathering place for the mission staff. The exposed wood along the walls and the ceiling felt like a summer camp building. Red and white checkered tablecloths imparted a home feeling. The wooden walls and simple interior had come to feel like home. The simple interior had come to feel warm and inviting. Father Stanley sat patiently at the long dining table that had become his office listening to Miguel Sanchez talk about his struggle to provide enough food for his family.

Miguel planted corn every year but when the Fall rains didn't come, the crop withered affecting everyone. Miguel needed help. The priest kept making notes on a small pad and listening intently.

"Padre," Miguel begged. "Can you help me?"

"I grew up farming. Absolutely. I'll work on a new strategy for your crops. We can't have you hanging on to life by a thread. I think we can improve your situation."

Stanley knew their average yearly income was $50 and half the children died before they were six-years old. That desperate situation had to be reversed. His knowledge of farming could help formulate an answer.

"Oh, Padre." Miguel Sanchez clutched his wide-brimmed hat in front of him and began bowing up and down.

"None of that," Fr. Stanley said. "I'm your friend. Come back in a day or two and we'll see where we can begin."

"*Si, si*," Miguel Sanchez started bowing again as he backed out of the room.

Fr. Stanley smiled as he prepared for the next person to show up.

The first team who had come down from America had built the two-story rectory. Long after they left, their contribution provided him a home. Periodically, smoke rolled up from the volcanos, but that only added to the picturesque nature of the land. Three large volcanos surrounded the town and towered up into the sky. Father Tom Stafford had helped build a radio station and that added much to their mission. The Indians could hear Mass in their native language now. Stanley now found that he was needed to help keep the "Voice of Atitlan" on the air. He was still working much of the time on a hospital construction project on the edge of the village. Most difficult of all, he continued trying to learn two new languages.

When he first arrived, Fr. Stanley found his first job was repairing the bathroom floor in the women's wing of the rectory complex. As he began attempting to find his place among the team from the United States, he sensed tension with some of the more scholarly extroverts that had been fired up by the changes that had come out of Vatican II. Their interest was in creating change in the church and debating new ideas. Stan listened but felt somewhat alienated from their heated discussions. He was a conservative Catholic who saw his role as helping the people more than debating new approaches. He felt his time was better spent in the hospital helping the sisters care for the broken when the Tz'utuijil people hobbled in for care. One evening the differences came to a head in a discussion around the wooden tables.

The Jesuit and academic professionals sat around the dining room discussing what approach the nuns should take to be correctly involved in the life and needs of the Tz'utuijil. Fr. Stanley sat to the back of the dining hall listening.

"We've got to show them the way," Father Alexander said. "They are primitive people who just don't know what we can bring them. They need to listen to us."

"He's right," Sister Elizabeth said. "We are living in a time of catastrophic change. We can help these Indians become part of something new that is breaking out everywhere. The Second Vatican Council taught us to cast aside the old methods, the old language, and catch up with the Twentieth Century."

"I don't see it that way at all," John Camp broke in. "I know I'm a layperson, but I didn't come down here to feed these people 'the American way.' I came to be their friend and help them with the problems they struggle with each day. Forget all that revolutionary talk."

"I strongly agree," a nun shouted from the rear of the dining hall.

"Now just a minute!" Father Alexander's voice took on a condescending tone. "*We* have studied the new results of the Council that call for change. That's what we are trying to bring, bone fide renewal. We must respect the new directions. The winds of the future are blowing. You must stand in the winds of change."

"I don't think my purpose is to be a spokesperson for that Council," Sister Priscilla said. "My calling is to help the suffering. You guys can argue theology all day, but I am here to be with the indigenous people."

The disagreement went back and forward, seemingly without end. The two sides simply had very different perspectives and they weren't budging. Where the debate would go wasn't clear, but the deep division of opinion was. The staff were digging their heels into their different approaches.

Father Stanley sat in the back listening quietly and saying nothing. The discussion became even more heated as the Jesuit archeologists and Fr. Alexander pushed for direct engagement in teaching the Indians how things should be done while others in the group believed they should be working with the Tz'utuijil in a partnership approach, helping them refine the directions that were natural to them. Fr. Stanley quickly saw that they were a house divided and the problem wasn't going to get any better quickly. Without saying anything, he got up and quietly withdrew to his room.

For a long time, Stanley sat on the bed and thought about the wrangling and arguing that he had heard. When he attended several seminaries, he had struggled with Latin, Logic, and didn't like some of the abstract philosophical courses. It wasn't that he didn't understand the issues; they simply weren't particularly important in his world. A farm boy is practical, basic, and forthright. Much of what he heard when the philosophical footballs were being kicked around seemed irrelevant to his interest. The disagreements down in the dining hall were of that order.

He got up and rolled down his blanket, preparing to go to bed. Stanley turned out the lights and stared into the darkness. They were all good people with different points of view. Still, he couldn't see a positive or immediate solution to the struggle.

***

During the next few days, Fr. Rother returned to helping complete a hospital building on the edge of the village. He still found time to talk with the natives when they came to the rectory. Between hammering nails and listening to problems, he was able to push the disagreements aside. Almost.

Sister Anne walked through the 2x4's that would eventually be an entry and stopped. He laid his hammer down and smiled.

"I have a question for you," she began. "I don't like the direction that some of the leadership is trying to take. Are we evangelizing these people or materializing them? When I hear some of the dogmatic statements being made these days, I am worried about what we are doing for these folks. Are we really helping them for their own good?"

Stanley took a deep breath. "I understand."

"Well, are we helping them maximize their own culture or trying to turn them into middle-class Americans? I certainly know where that is going!"

"What do you mean?"

"I've studied what happened to Indians in America. In those great attempts to "Americanize" them, we produced a mass of drunks and dispossessed. We profoundly injured them."

"What are you going to do?" he asked.

"I'm thinking about leaving the rectory and moving in with the people in the town. I want to be one of them."

"I understand Father Stafford is going to start wearing the *traije,* the traditional Tz'utuijil native dress of the men. He told me that he is about to move out of the rectory and into the village as a way of expressing his disapproval of where mission policy is going."

Sister Anne shook her head in disgust. "Fr. Stanley, I want to know where you stand."

"I abhor disagreement and confrontation. However, I came down here to help the people, not debate theological doctrine. I'm going to stand with the people."

"Good." Sister Ann smiled for the first time. "That's what I thought you'd say, Stan. You're a kind man and we need more kindness around here."

Fr. Stanley picked up his hammer. "I'm a rather practical person. I guess I'm going to keep on trying to help these local folks."

18

The controversy didn't subside during the next few months. Discussions became even more heated, but Stanley stayed on the sidelines. Several more of the staff declared they were ready to move into the town with the people to declare their support of the Indians. The mission team leader disagreed with that idea and many of the Indians expressed their opinion that the Americans ought to stay in the rectory. The idea faded, but the tension remained. Fr. Stanley kept his focus on finishing building the hospital complex.

Abruptly, a measles epidemic broke out. The mission staff made frantic efforts to fight the disease that spread rapidly among the children. The battle raged day and night. Stanley was swept along in the fight to stop the vicious attacks of the illness.

"Father," the small woman struggled to walk into one of the unfinished rooms of the hospital where he was working. "My child," she cried. "My child has the dread disease. She peeled back the *scarf* covering his face. The blank eyes stared into a void in an empty gaze. "Please pray for him."

Father Stanley felt tears starting to surge forward. He spread the covering back over the child's face and placed his hand gently on the little chest and prayed spontaneously for the mother and child. When he finished, the little woman trudged out of the hospital, carrying her lifeless child toward the cemetery where another priest stood by a freshly dug grave.

Stanley stood in the door for a long time. The epidemic would take many more lives before it was over. They had to get the hospital finished. Supplies were lacking. Technical equipment had to be sent in. Demand would not stop. Forget the intellectual disagreements.

By the time the scourge had passed, sixty children had died.

***

Fr. Rother increased his efforts to complete the hospital rooms. He and the Tz'utuijil workers laid all the concrete blocks in the walls. Slowly, the twenty-one rooms came together. Floors were finished and windows put in place. Stanley even put in all the wiring and wall plugs, the job of a professional electrician. Perhaps, the most difficult part of the project he and one of the natives worked on was digging a 90-foot water well. Never complaining, he and the Tz'utuijil helper worked tirelessly. His skills learned from years on a farm had never found a better and more important use. Often, he dropped into bed at night so exhausted from the day's efforts that he fell asleep instantly.

For the first time in the history of these descendants of the ancient Mayans, they had a hospital with an operating room, a lab, a radiology department and a facility with twenty-one beds. The memory of those sixty children would be forever served by this adequately equipped healing center.

Once the building was completed, Stanley turned his attention to further language development. Along with some sisters and other clergy, he checked in at the Guatemalan American Institute for intense training to learn Spanish. For twenty-four hours a day, learning the language became the total obsession of the students. As always, Stanley struggled with languages, but he didn't give up. after four months of continuous work, he still labored, but did find it easier to understand the Spanish the way the Tz'utuijil's spoke. Stanley began to find it more accessible to pick up the Indian's native language.

During his time at the Institute, he learned there were twenty-two separate languages that had evolved from the same source. The Mayan civilization reached its height around 1,000 BCE and then began to decline. When the Spaniards came, the Mayans split up into various groups. Even though impacted by Spanish evangelization efforts, they had retained much of the ancient culture and customs. The more Stanley learned, the more he respected these native people. They had a rich heritage to be proud of. Slowly but surely, he was learning to say Mass in their language.

With his developing language skills, Fr. Stanley was placed in charge of the Cerro de Oro parish about five miles from Santiago Atitlan where the village church sat close to the lake. Each week over 80 families showed up for Mass. On Friday night, he met with the Tz'utuijil Indians and discussed the next day's scripture lessons with anyone who came. Most did.

When Sunday morning came, the villagers filed into the church reverently and listened to the priest preach his sermon in Spanish and then do the liturgy in their language. Fr. Stanley found the services exhilarating. The parish flourished.

One of the highlights of his Cerro de Oro experience came during Holy Week. He was sitting by the altar as the reader recited the portion that described the crucifixion and death of Jesus. No one made a sound. The readers' voice echoed across the church. "Jesus cried out with a loud voice, 'Father, into your hands I commit my spirit.' When he had said this, he breathed his last."

At that moment the doors at the back of the church swung open. Men silently walked down the aisle carrying a large coffin. The sound of their sandals slapping against the cement floor echoed across the packed sanctuary. At the front, they solemnly set the casket in the center of the church. Another Indian came forward carrying a black chasuble. He covered the head of the casket in black with great reverence. The men turned and walked slowly to the back of the sanctuary, knowing that they had graphically proclaimed the real death of Christ their high priest.

Fr. Stanley watched, moved by what he had seen. These people certainly took their faith seriously. He knew that at 4 a.m., men from the church would start walking through the village singing, "Alleluia, Christ the Lord is risen." The people would rise and hurry to the church for the Easter morning Mass celebrating the resurrection. With the same dignity, they would remove the black chasuble and take the lid off the casket. A white sheet would be placed inside. Women would carry in lilies to be placed around the sides with the paschal candle at the head. The people would know Christ is risen.

This year the people elected to make a pilgrimage to the top of Cerro de Oro, or the Hill of gold. Stanley knew the custom resonated with their Mayan past. The blending of the old way and the new path would unfold as the sun came up. The Mayans had worshipped the sun as the source of life, but now the sun's coming up meant Jesus Christ had risen victorious from the tomb.

"As we stand here on this dawn," Stanley explained. "Let us renew our baptismal vows. Our lives have been restored as surely as the new day has begun." He started walking through the crowd, sprinkling water on their heads. Fr. Stanley murmured his own prayer as he moved through the throng.

One of the women tugged at his alb. "Thank you. Bless you, Father."

19

1971

One morning the sun didn't seem to come up. When the villagers peered into the sky, they realized it was not clouds, but smoke that blotted out the sun's rays. During the night, one of the volcanoes had come to life. Since Atitlan was located in a niche between three towering volcanos, their location remained fragile. Volcano Fuego began sending ash drifting across the house tops and the air took on an acid, burning smell. Eruptions were nothing new to the natives and they went about their business as usual.

With the smell of smoke looming in the air, Fr. Stanley walked into the village. A man named Pedro and a little boy were coming toward him. "What do you think of the volcanic activity?"

Pedro stopped and smiled. "I guess we have made the gods angry who live in the fire." The little boy tugged at Stanley's hand.

"You really think so?" Stanley reached down and picked up the child. He giggled and pulled at Stanley's beard.

"No," the native laughed, "but that's what the people once believed. Our ancestors were taken with fire and thought it carried evil spirits. You have taught us different."

Fr. Stanley laughed. "Good. How long do you think this eruption will last, Pedro?"

"Can't say. We never know. Maybe a few days. Maybe a month. Maybe longer."

The little boy started tickling Stanley's neck. He laughed and sat him on the ground. "Well, Pedro, keep your head covered." They shook hands and walked on.

He thought about how things had changed. So many of the mission staff had left. Fr. Tom Stafford and been called back to America. Other priests and some of the Sisters had come and gone. Of course, the tensions over a difference of opinion about how to approach the natives had cooled and that was good. He loved the Cerro de Oro parish and the work remained highly meaningful. Maybe the volcanic smoke and fire mean nothing. Certainly, was good to hear Pedro joke about the ancient's beliefs that evil spirits lived in fire. Good things were happening.

"Padre!" an excited woman called from the doorway of the *Officina Postal,* the post office. "Padre Francisco, a Special Delivery letter has just arrived for you."

"Me?" Fr. *Stanley frowned.* "Who in the world would send me such a letter?"

"*Yo no se?"* the postmistress shrugged and handed him a specially marked envelope.

"Good heavens," Stanley started opening the letter. "It's from my family in America."

"America?" the woman said with a note of wonder in her voice. "America! Muy bueno!"

Fr. Stanley smiled and sat down on the ancient worn bench standing against the wall. "I'll read it right now."

The postmistress walked back inside. Seldom, if ever, did a Special Delivery letter or package come from America. She seemed to be duly impressed with herself for having gotten it in his hands so quickly.

The clouds of smoke kept the sun from bearing down so reading would be more pleasant. Stanley opened the specially stamped envelope.

"Dear Son,

We have been so concerned over what is happening to your brother Jim. He has been diagnosed with leukemia. Of course, his wife and children are scared to death. The prognosis is bleak. We are all frightened for their future.

At this time, I don't think you should come home, but you must pray. Please pray constantly. Jim is receiving excellent medical care and everything possible is being done for him. Your Sister Marita has asked her students to pray for him as well.

We bleed the blood of Jesus for Jim. We know you will do the same.

Your mother

Stan's hand started to shake, and he clenched his teeth. "Why couldn't it have been me? I have no family. Oh, Lord. Please be with my dear brother Jim. For a long time, Stanley sat on the bench, clenching the letter. The volcano no longer seemed to be a problem.

***

During the next two days, the thought of his brother's illness haunted him. Stanley sat at the dining room table drinking coffee and thinking about Jim. Periodically, he launched into a prayer of intercession. Jim had always been such a good, faithful guy and he loved him. Over and over, he thought about why it couldn't have been him. Here he was in far off Guatemala while the entire family struggled in Oklahoma.

"Father Stanley!" the Sister rushed across the dining hall. "Have I ever got a surprise for you."

Her call jarred him out of his reverie. Sister Anna was one of the mission volunteers. He stood.

"You have a visitor that has come all the way from the United States to see you. She just arrived."

"What? Stan looked around the room but didn't see anyone. "What are you talking about?"

The door swung open, and Sister Clarissa Tenbrink walked in.

"Sister!" Stanley rushed over to her.

"Well, well. Here's my fifth-grade boy out here in the middle of a jungle!"

"You couldn't have come at a more important time," Stanley said.

"I just wanted to make sure you were behaving yourself."

Stan laughed. "Always the teacher."

Sister Clarissa smiled. "Always your mentor."

"You certainly have been that."

"Why is this time so important, Stan?"

"Please sit down." He pointed to the bench. "I have a letter that I received only a couple of days ago." Stanley handed her the paper. "I think this says it all."

Sister Clarissa started glancing at the letter. Then she stopped and read it again much more slowly. "Oh, my." She handed it back to him. "I see," she said slowly.

Stanley sat there shaking his head. "I am devastated and just don't know what to do. It's all so painful."

"My son," the nun said. "At important times in the past, I have encouraged you and given you words that I felt the Holy Spirit was directing. I pray so again. During your seminary day when everything seemed so dark, you realized you couldn't quit, and another door opened unexpectedly. This is no different. You must trust God for the answer just as you did in San Antonio. You must trust God to take care of Jim just as He has taken care of you. Our heavenly Father will do so."

Stan bit his lip. "Thank you," he mumbled. "I needed to hear that word."

Because we are about God's business doesn't mean we are exempt from the struggles that go on in the world every day. We are just the hand of God remains on us as it will on your brother Jim. Stanley, keep on trusting, trusting every moment of every hour."

Fr. Stan reached for her hand and squeezed it. "Thank you, Sister Clarissa. Once again, your voice has broken through the darkness and brought me hope."

***

During the next couple of days, Fr. Stanley showed Sister Clarissa their grounds, the hospital, and took her over to Corro de

Oro. As her visit came to an end, she reminded him that he was fulfilling a destiny she always believed he had. Like a breath of fresh air from home, Sister Clarissa's visit helped him pull through another dark time. Whatever happened, he knew the hand of God would be on his brother. When he waved goodbye, Stanley's last words were "Please, hurry back soon." And then Sister Clarissa was gone.

Life returned to the predictable pattern that absorbed almost every moment of Father Stanley's time. The staff had gathered for supper and were seated around the room in their usual places. As he always did, Stanley sat to the back of the room. Chatting with the Sister seating across from him, as usual he asked how they had spent the day. Everyone had a story.

"Excuse me," Father Jude Pansini, the new director of the mission project, called for everyone to quiet down. He tapped on a glass with his fork. "I just received an important message from the United States. Many of you will find this to be personal. I am sorry and saddened to announce that our beloved Bishop Victor Reed has died."

Stanley felt like his heart had stopped for a moment. This man who had been his mentor, his advocate, his friend was gone. Once more the dark clouds descended. He sat there in silence, staring down at the red and white checkered tablecloth. No one spoke.

"Let us pray," Father Pansini said and began the intercessions.

Stanley remained subdued in thought to himself. Volcano Fuego has erupted again.

20

Father Rother walked through the rows of corn with Miguel Sanchez behind him. Periodically, the priest stopped and inspected an ear of corn sticking out of the stalks. The crop had done much, much better than in previous years. The Sanchez family would be blessed with better nutrition during the coming winter. Fr. Stanley's changes in managing the land and the time of planting had paid off.

"See, Padre," Miguel said. "My crop has prospered because of what you taught us."

The two men sat down on an old tree trunk at the edge of the field. Miguel Sanchez took off his wide-brimmed hat and took another long look over the field.

"Padre Aplas, we are grateful. You have helped my people so much. The new hospital is a gift from God and now the crop is greatly improved." He paused and thought for a moment. "Perhaps, there is something that I can tell you that will be of help to you and your friends from America. I'm sure you know nothing about the *cofradis.*"

Stanley shook his head. Never heard the word before."

"You would probably call them something more like a confraternity. These people are hidden from you, but they exist to preserve something of our Mayan heritage by hiding their beliefs behind Catholic doctrine."

The priest frowned. "What? I don't understand?"

The *cofradias* appear to be devoted to the many *santos*, saints, that have statues or pictures in the churches. However, they only use the name of the saint to cover old Mayan beliefs. I'm sure you've never head of *Itzamna* the Creator of the rain god *Chac*. Then there is the goddess of fertility *Ix Chel*, and the gods of death, *Ah Puch* and *Akan*. These names are strange to you? No?"

Fr. Stanley shook his head. "I'm sure none of the missionaries have ever heard any of this. No, no. We know nothing about what you are saying."

"For centuries before the Spanish came, our people believed in as many as 200 gods. After the invaders made us change our religion, the *cofradias* simply changed the name of the gods to the name of the saints. They blended into the church doing activities like helping with vestments or singing in the choir. *Cofradia* are everywhere. Often, they keep the keys to the church."

Stanley's mouth dropped. "I-I don't think any of our team ever had a clue. We have been pulled into this system with no idea what was going on."

Miguel shook his head. "Of course. We never speak about the *cofradias* outside of our immediate families. Some people believe in them, many others don't."

"They are everywhere?"

"In some places there are abandoned churches they have taken over. From the outside, the buildings look like an everyday church. Inside the old church is totally different. Straw covers the floor, and the entire building is surrounded by statues and pictures of an endless number of saints. Candles burn in front of these shrines so that the entire building is filled with smoke. A strange smell of burning wax and the vapors permeated the entire church. These places are shrines to ancient gods like Misty Sky. In the old days he was most often illustrated as an ancient man, stooped with age, with a prominent, beaked nose and a sunken, toothless mouth. Occasionally pictured smoking a cigar, this god is also associated with tobacco, jaguars and caves. See what I mean?"

Stanley stared. Finally, shaking his head he said, "I almost can't believe my ears. This system is what we have faced without knowing it even existed?"

"After the Spanish were run out, we had no spiritual leadership from the Church for a hundred years. No one challenged the system during this time. People took it for granted."

Fr. Stanley took a deep breath. "We will get nowhere if we attack these ideas head on. We will have to take a more cautious path for the moment, but I must make our people aware of the problem. We probably have *cofradia* working in the hospital."

"You do," Miguel said solemnly. "Believe me. You do. Have you ever noticed in some of the homes a little statue with a wooden face smoking a cigar?"

"Yes. Yes, I've seen several. Thought they were souvenirs of some kind."

"You were looking at Maximon. He isn't representative of any saint but is an idol unto himself. The people sometimes bring Maximon out during Holy Week. This idol was always a big problem."

"Problem?" Stanley shook his head. "Problem indeed!"

***

Stanley had walked down the long road back to the village by himself. He couldn't get the information Miguel Sanchez had given him off of his mind. He had to admire the ingenuity and cleverness of the Mayans to develop such a system that appeared to be in compliance while subverting the missionary intents of the Spanish. To confront this infection head on would only create resistance. The missionaries must be cautious in how they respond.

Certainly, this Maximon idol must never be allowed entry into a church. Still, the hunk of wood must be treated carefully to eventually defeat this ancient curse. The job will not be easy.

Fr. Rother reached the missionary compound and walked into the dining hall. To his surprise, a good group had already assembled. "What's going on?"

"A meeting has been called," one of the Sisters said. "I'm not sure what the situation is."

"Ever heard of Maximon?" he asked.

The Sister frowned. "Is that a drug or something?"

Fr. Stanley's face hardened. "That's one way to put it… a drug to anaesthetize believers."

"What?" The sister grimaced. "I don't understand?"

"I'll explain the problem to the whole team in a few minutes. Ever see a strange looking statue smoking a cigar in any of the natives' homes?

"Well, come to think of it. I've seen several of those little figurines."

Fr. Stanley raised an eyebrow. "You've met Maximon."

The Sister's eyebrow raised, and she shook her head. "Sounds like Halloween."

The side door opened, and Father Pansini walked in with his hand raised. "I have an important announcement. Word has just come that our deceased friend Bishop Victor Reed has been succeeded. The new Bishop is John Raphael Quinn. A native of California, Bishop Quinn is now the fifth bishop of the Diocese of Oklahoma. Oklahoma will be divided into two dioceses. Bishop Quinn will become the Archbishop of the Archdiocese of Oklahoma City. The Diocese of Tulsa will received a new bishop. He sends his greeting to our mission here in Atitlan."

The Sister turned to Fr. Stanley. "Do you know this man?"

"No," he said. "Not at all."

The mission began to talk, buzzing about the change. Stanley sat quietly, listening. Finally, he stood and held up his hand. The room became quiet.

"I'm sure we will all pray for the success and blessing of our new Bishop. I am certain Bishop Quinn will be excellent. However, I have a different message that I need to convey tonight. I have discovered that we have an enemy in our midst."

Across the dining hall a low rumble of concern echoed. He waited until everyone quieted down. "His name is Maximon.

21

1975

The Archbishop's airplane circled above the lush green valley with Volcano Fuego spouting fire and ash. Archbishop John Quinn watched streams of lava flowing down the side of the mountain. Swirls of debris blew up into the air as the fiery eruption continued exploding below.

The Archbishop turned to his assistant. "To stay down there working with such a threatening problem hanging overhead takes considerable patience and personal serenity. I am somewhat surprised that Fr. Rother is still there under the circumstances."

"They tell me that he is a man of considerable endurance. One of the Sisters reported that Stanley Rother had a gentle graciousness about him."

"Hmm." Archbishop Quinn looked out the window again. "They say the town is rather primitive."

"The level of malnutrition is high. People struggle to survive. There's one light bulb in the whole village and that's in the center of town near the church. I'd say that's primitive."

"I guess so. Do you know why Fr. Rother accepted this assignment? What did he come here to do."

"I don't think he came *to do* anything. Rather, Fr. Stanley came *to be* there. His gift seems to be recognizing what needs to be done and taking care of the matter. With that mindset, he has produced an extraordinary amount of change … building a hospital … producing a school …changing farming habits for the good. That sort of thing."

Archbishop Quinn looked out the window again. "Impressive."

****

The day had proved productive as the archbishop toured the city and the rectory grounds. With an interpreter at his side, he talked with the people and listened to their responses. During the noon hour, Archbishop Quinn received the reports on the activities of the mission. Early in the afternoon, he began reviewing the sheets of paper that kept a tally of the activities of the mission. Reading them slowly, he carefully assessed the numbers. The door opened and Fr. Stanley walked in.

The archbishop smiled. "Sit down, Father Rother. I wanted to talk with you about these numbers."

"Yes, sir."

"I see that 649 babies were baptized in Lake Atitlan. That is an exceptional number for a mission station."

"The people have been responsive," the priest said.

"Then 150 children took their first communion. I further note that 2,000 Holy Communions were distributed. That's something larger than simply having cooperative or passive parishioners. In addition, I know that the mission staff has been significantly reduced over the past couple of years. Priests and nuns returned to America while you stayed. In fact, you alone now preside over the entire liturgical life of the mission. Something you are doing completely on your own."

Fr. Stanley shrugged. "Well, yes."

Archbishop Quinn leaned back in his chair and studied this man standing before him. Stanley had on a simple pullover T-shirt and faded blue slacks. The garment around his neck was of exactly the same weave that all the natives wore. He looked more like one of the people than a priest.

"I am highly impressed," Archbishop Quinn said. "You are to be more than commended. You have taken on a significant load and performed admirably. Your Church thanks you."

Father Stanley smiled. "We simply try to do our best. We have problems from time to time, but we keep on going."

The archbishop looked at him thoughtfully. "Keep on doing what you are doing. I also see that you have organized the 110 acres of land owned by the mission into a farming co-op. The land is divided into parcels worked by 45 natives. How is this project doing?"

A broad smile broke across the priest's face. "We have made important progress. Changing the fertilization process has made a significant difference in production. Right now, we are experimenting with three types of new corn. I am going to have these farmers try raising wheat and soybeans. The reports in your hands noted that we have lowered the infant mortality rate and the hospital is part of that success. I believe we've made three additional months of food possible."

My assistant told me that he noticed this morning when you walked through the fields, many of the workers rushed up to kiss your hand."

Fr. Stanley shook his head. "I don't encourage that practice, Archbishop."

My assistant also noticed that now there are many babies named Francisco or Alpas, named after you."

Stanley just smiled.

"Those are high honors, Fr. Rother. The people not only respect you but love and care about you. You can be proud."

"I'm only doing my job."

"Oh, not much, much more. You have given much more attention to developing and expanding the work of this mission."

Stanley smiled again, nodded, and walked out.

***

Archbishop Quinn and his assistant walked across the tarmac toward the airplane that would take them back to the United States. The line was already forming for boarding.

"An important visit," the archbishop said. "We must make sure our people understand the significant work going on here."

"I was certainly impressed. Did you notice how thin Rother's face was?"

"I did think he looked a little drawn," the archbishop said. "We didn't discuss it."

"I learned that he regularly visits the natives' homes, blesses their houses with dirt floors, and eats with them. Of course, the food has many problems, but he doesn't want to offend the people. As a result, this priest gets sick much of the time. That's the problem."

The archbishop stopped and looked at the assistant. "He never mentioned any of this."

One of the nurses told me that infectious hepatitis is rampant around here."

"God help Stanley Rother," the archbishop said and continued walking to the airplane.

The commercial airplane sped down the runway and lifted into the air. Archbishop Quinn sat next to the window as the large airplane circled and then lifted above the jungle. Off in the distance, the smoke was still circling up from Volcano Fuego. Fr. Rother would be going about his business working with the people."

"God be with you, Stanley," Archbishop Quinn mumbled under his breath. "Bless you."

22

With new insight into the hidden religious customs of some of the natives, the missionary enterprise had a new understanding of what they were facing. The concealed ancient customs of the Mayans had to be confronted in various ways. Father Stanley continued greeting the *confriads* like old friends, not leaving a hint of his actual feelings about what they represented. Though slow, progress was being made.

Volunteers frequently dropped in to help the mission. In the late winter, Alice Yeats came in from the United States with a desire to help the natives. Fr. Stanley began taking her with him when he visited the homes. Generally, his sick calls were made in the late afternoon or evening. Alice found climbing steep stone steps to be a challenge but stayed with the task. Often she sat in a corner and watched the priest minister to the infirm.

"Tonight, we are going to the house of Tomas," Fr. Stanley told Alice. "Tomas is dying."

Alice took a deep breath and stiffened. "I see," she said slowly.

"The people jokingly called Tomas 'the bishop' because he liked to walk behind me in public processions. Interesting guy. Tomas is important in the village."

"Be interesting to meet him," Alice said.

Stanley and Alice walked through the winding streets of the village. Long shadows fell across their path. An enticing smell of cooking food rolled out of the windows of some of the houses. They kept walking.

"Here is the house of Tomas," the priest said. "His family will be expecting us. Just watch."

Alice nodded her compliance.

A few of the natives stood around the room. Candles had been placed on the table, sending a scent of burning wax across the small bedroom. Alice found a small simple chair and sat to one side. Tomas lay motionless, covered by a dirty white blanket. No one spoke.

Father Stanley placed a simple stole around his neck and began the prayers by first making the sign of the Cross over Tomas. Finally, he pulled out a bottle of anointing oil. Once more the priest made the sign of the Cross and started making another Cross on the dying man's forehead with the oil.

Tomas shot straight up in the bed as if a renewing shot of vitality had just raced through his veins. His eyes popped open, and he looked straight into Fr. Stanley's eyes.

Alice leaned forward in her chair not believing what she was seeing.

Tomas put his hands on the priest's head and started shouting in Tz'utuijil. The room became electric. As abruptly as he had begun, Tomas fell back on the bed. His eyes closed. The priest stood there not moving. Tomas stopped breathing.

Alice glanced at Fr. Stanley and saw his eyes watering. She started backing away and slipped through the door to wait outside.

Leaning against the wall, Alice tried to compose herself, but couldn't stop crying. Never had she seen such a thing. While death had only been an idea in the back of her mind, the fact had now become a staggering reality. The sight was almost more than she could take.

After a few minutes, Stanley came out and closed the door behind him. He looked at Alice and offered her his handkerchief.

"I've never seen anything like that." She wiped the tears from her eyes. "What did he say to you when he sat up in bed?"

"I can't report his confession and even if I did, I'd be too embarrassed. Those were his last words."

For a long time, they walked quietly through the narrow streets back to the rectory. Finally, Alice said, "This has been one of the most profound experiences of my life."

They walked on silently.

***

The next morning, the missions team gathered for breakfast, talking, chatting, the usual thoughts and agenda for the day. As always, Stanley sat in his usual place, listening, responding.

Eventually, one of the Carmelite sisters came in holding a canvas sack. "Mail call!" she called out and began reading off names on the letters she pulled out of the bag. People came forward to get their letters or small packages.

"Here's one for Father Rother," she said.

Stanley picked up the small envelope and opened it. For a moment, he read the letter. "That's thoughtful."

"What is it?" Alice Yeats asked.

"Hmm. A check for $500. The lady wants me to buy new clothes." Stan shrugged. "I don't need any new clothes." He handed the check to the Sister that handled the funds. "Put that in the account for the people. I don't need clothes." He tucked his small pipe in his shirt pocket. "Think I'll take a short walk." Stanley started toward the door.

Alice Yeats watched him disappear. "He dresses so humbly," she said to the Sister next to her. "I thought I lived a simple life, but I've sure learned new lessons in the meaning of sincere austerity. I've been challenged."

"Wait!" the Carmelite Sister called out. "I missed a special delivery letter that got mixed in with some of the small packages down at the bottom. "Someone go get Fr. Rother. It's for him."

Alice Yeats darted out the door. "Father Stanley!" she yelled as loudly as possible. "Come back! You've got another important letter!"

Down the street, he turned. For a moment the priest stared and then started back.

When he walked in, the Sister apologized for missing the letter. Obviously, it must be important. Stanley took the specially stamped envelope and sat down. Everyone around the table watched.

Stanley begam reading. His face froze. His hand began to tremble. The letter tumbled to the floor.

Alice swept up the small pink paper and placed it on the table. Tears had begun running down Stanley's cheeks and he didn't seem to be able to speak. She glanced at the letter.

Dear Son,

 I don't know how to tell you. Today your brother Jim died of Leukemia.

 The doctors did all they could, but nothing stopped the dread disease.

 His wife Mary Lou and the boys Kenneth and Matt are having an extremely difficult time.

 We know you cannot possibly get back in time for the funeral Mass and the burial, but you can help all of us in your prayers. We will miss you. Keep praying.

 Love,

  Your mother

Stanley turned and rushed out of the dining hall. The remaining staff stared, unable to understand his departure. Alice held up the letter. "I think Stan would want all of us to know what's happened. He's going to need our support."

A murmur of affirmation went around the room.

"Stan's brother died," Alice said. "Let's all pray."

23

The days of grief were not easy to endure. The mission staff prayed and were sensitive to Stanley's struggle. Jim Rother had been a buddy, a friend, a brother. Stanley said little but the strain was written on his face. He often took long walks alone. The beauty of the forest and the affection of the people lifted him. Letters came from Sister Marita, and he answered her, pouring out his heart. Again and again, he thought about his sister-in-law Mary Lou and her sons Kenneth and Matt. Most of all, they felt the sting of the loss. When Holy Week came, his parents Franz and Gertrude journeyed to Guatemala and that lifted him.

In the late spring, Sister Marita volunteered to come to Santiago Atitlan. Being with his sister once again infused new joy into Stanley's life. She came as a representative of her community, the Adorers of the Blood of Christ, ready to do whatever would help. The hospital and the nutrition station profited from her help and assistance. In the evening, she joined Fr. Stanley on his long walks. Sister Marita walked out of the hospital and found her brother waiting for their afternoon walk.

"Did you do any good today?" Stanley chided her.

"I doubt it," Sister Marita shot back and fell in with his pace.

"Are you enjoying being here?" Stan asked.

"I am amazed. You have done so much. I think my next job is to help with indexing baptisms and wedding registries of the parish. Honestly, it's truly been fun being part of all that this mission does."

"Since we started way back in the Sixties, many clergy and volunteers have come down to help. Got the radio station running. The church renewed. Hospital built. I think the people are most grateful."

"You're too modest. I've seen you with the indigenous people. You are their true friend, and the children adore you."

Stanley laughed. "Oh, but I do love the kids. They are my buddies. Love to climb all over me." He chuckled again. "Yeah, the little ones like to pull on my legs. Quite a show, Betty Mae."

"You can't help calling me your little sister."

"Afraid so. By the way. I have access to a small airplane. How'd you like to take a ride and see what the environs look like from the air?"

"Really? I'd be thrilled to death."

"Let's go!"

***

The Piper Cub roared down the runway and quickly lifted into the air. Circling above the tree covered jungle and lush greenery obscuring the ground, the sight was stunning. The airplane swooped down closer to the treetops. Sister Marita could see what many called the Sun Temple rising high up above surrounding trees.

"Archeologists believe there are probably 3,000 remains of some kind of buildings that are the remanent of an ancient city once called *Yax Mutal.*" Stanley explained. "Some of the Tikal buildings date back to the fourth Century B.C., long before any Europeans arrived. Over a thousand years ago, the Mayans had a sophisticated society. Quite an achievement."

"Wow!" Sister Marita said. "What an amazing story."

"Back then the Mayans developed a powerful kingdom and ruled this area in Guatemala," he continued. "As we work with them, we try to respect what they once were. The Indians have a significant history."

Sister Marita nodded knowingly. "An important past."

The airplane continued surveying the countryside. Additional Mayan temples rose up high out of the surrounding jungle. Finally, they turned back to the base.

"We've got to get back," Stanley said. "I have a late afternoon Mass and the people will be gathering. You'll find the congregation to be interesting."

Sister Maria smiled. "Let's go."

***

Many of the natives had already filed into the church when Sister Marita walked in. Some were still kneeling when she slipped into the pew. An Indian boy, the acolyte of the day, lit the candles on the altar. The processional hymn began, and everyone stood. Wearing his usual white alb and native stole, Fr. Stanley came down the aisle behind the crucifix. As the Mass started to unfold, Sister Marita watched every aspect of the worship with a critical eye. Not suspicious, she was devoted to the liturgy, the prayers, the flow of worship and wanted each detail to be right. Since her brother was the priest, Sister Marita maintained a careful observation of what he said and did. Stanley had provided an interpreter who sat beside her whispering what the Tz'utuijil words meant.

As Sister Marita watched, her brother seemed to slip into another world. Profoundly reverent, he appeared almost swept away as he repeated the words of the liturgy. There was nothing mechanical in how he moved from one part of the liturgy to another. Fr. Stanley simply flowed with the order of worship. She looked around the sanctuary and could see that the people had caught the same spirit of praise. The Indians had been pulled into the meaning of the Mass.

Fr. Stanley walked to the pulpit for the homily. For a few moments he stood there silently, then he began to speak in a certain and forceful voice. On this day, he was explaining the mystical Body of Christ inherent in the Eucharist. The bread, the wine became the sacramental presence of Jesus Christ in the form of bread and wine in the sanctuary, in the participants. The priest encouraged the people to allow the body of Christ now in them to do His work in the world, to bring wholeness to the broken, to show forth in unconditional love. When he finished, he stood silently behind the pulpit for a long time, and then slipped away to the chair.

Sister Marita felt a lump arise in her throat. Yes, Stanley was her brother, but before her eyes he had become the image of Christ.

24

In the middle of the night, a strange sound woke Stanley. The low-grade rumble began shaking the rectory. Stanley felt his bed start to shake slightly and then the vibration increased, sending the bed sliding across the floor. He sat up and tried to fight off the disorienting, bizarre sensation. The entire room began to move. Everyone knew Guatemala had always been earthquake country, but no one thought much of it. Little tremors now and then were to be expected. Then the entire rectory building shook violently.

Stanley leaped out of bed and pulled his pants on. Just as he reached for his belt, he fell backward. Grabbing for the bedstead, he tumbled on top of the blanket. The entire world seemed to be moving beneath his feet. Getting out of the house would be vital to prevent being crushed by a falling roof or hit by descending beams. Crawling seemed to be the most reasonable way out. Stanley slowly inched through the doorway and out on the porch, but the ground kept shaking.

Some of the sisters worked their way down the stairs. Wrapped in bathrobes, they began assembling out in the plaza. Sister Elizabeth led the way. The entire village began moving. For the first time, Stanley glanced at his wristwatch. To his surprise, it was only

3:00 in the morning. Here and there the light of candles began to appear in windows.

"Are you okay?" Stanley asked Sister Elizabeth.

"I-I think so," the nun stuttered. Her hair had tumbled over her face.

"Where are the others?"

The Sister pointed over her shoulder. "B-behind me ... I-I t-think ... I hope."

For a moment the ground stopped shaking. Two more women hurried through the door. "More are coming," Sister Anne shouted. "Never felt anything like this ... the world seems to be coming apart."

Another Sister staggered on to the porch. Once more the earth started to wrinkle. Everyone grabbed the person nearest to them and hung on. The shaking continued for several seconds and then stopped.

"We've got to get to the hospital," Sister Elizabeth said. "I'm sure people will be coming in."

"I'll get the radio station on." Stanley started walking toward the building. "We need to find out how widespread this earthquake has been. I'm sure other areas have been hit hard. Probably covered the entire country." He looked at his wristwatch again. "You know this tremor lasted quite a while."

"Felt like forever," Sister Anne said.

"There'll be aftershocks," Stan added. "We need to act fast before we get hit again."

The Sisters returned to the rectory to get dressed and get to their stations of service. The radio station stood not far away, and

Stanley knew what to do. In a short time, the entire mission outpost was mobilized.

***

The sun was just coming up when Fr. Stanley turned off the radio and put the phone down. It had been a long night, but what he had learned made it seem even longer. Putting the headset on the table, he walked outside to examine the church. He walked up the stairs and could see a few cracks that ran up the bell tower. Broken pieces of plaster were scattered on the veranda, but the ancient building had endured. The priest walked inside. Rays of morning sunlight fell across the sanctuary. He walked down the center aisle, looking closely at the floor and ceiling. Looked normal. Only a statue of Saint Joseph had toppled over. Stanley pushed the heavy structure back up and into place. A few dabs of paint here and there and no one would be able to tell the difference.

Satisfied that the Church of St. James the Apostle had endured the storm, Fr. Stanley returned to the rectory. Lights were already shining through the windows. Probably everyone had already spent the last few hours doing their emergency tasks. Sisters would have been working at the hospital during the last three hours. Stanley walked in and poured a cup of coffee. The staff were seated around the room chatting in quiet voices. He walked to the center of the room.

"I've got an initial report on what happened last night," Fr. Stanley said in a loud voice. "We got the best of it, but other cities are in ruins. Agua Escondido is only ten miles away, but they suffered severe devastation. Many were killed and injured. Roads and bridges into Guatemala City have been badly damaged and many are out. Landslides occurred and probably more will occur in the next few hours. I received a report from the capital that Los Amiates reported an earthquake of the magnitude of 7.5 along with great damage." Stanley stopped and shook his head. "Guatemala City really got whacked. Many have died and many more are injured. Houses have collapsed on top of the residents."

Sister Anne raised her hand. "What about Lake Atitlan? Earthquakes can do harm to such a body of water."

"Over the radio I received a response from Guatemala City that they are worried that the bottom of the lake could be cracked and create drainage problems. We'll have to watch the water level carefully."

"Do you have any information on what we should do next?" Sister Elizabeth asked.

"The capital wants us to put together a team of two doctors and two nurses to go with me over to the town of Patzun. Big, big problems over there. I don't know if we can get through right now but as soon as the sun is completely up, we must try. Patzun is only 18 miles away, but that doesn't mean anything right now. All we can do is load up and try to get in." For a few moments, Stanley couldn't talk. Finally, he said, "They think 1,000 people have already died in Patzun."

A gasp echoed across the room.

"We are going to need the help of the citizens in Santiago Atitlan. Some of you must go through the village gathering up supplies ... food ... tortillas ... boiled eggs ... food stuff like that ... we will need to share with the villages that are around us."

A young native priest stood up. "Father, I know that many people live down in the valleys. Those roads will probably be impassable even to donkeys. What will we do?"

"We will have to climb down the mountainside and carry the injured down by hand or on our backs. There is no other way."

"But you are the only one strong enough to carry a person out," the Indian priest said.

"We will just have to do what we can," Stanley said quietly.

***

The next morning a Sister struggled into Santiago Atitlan. She had walked eighteen miles in from the town of Chimaltenango. Sister Rosa found her way into the rectory and nearly collapsed at one of the tables. The staff gathered around her.

"We desperately need your help," Sister Rosa said. "The earthquake collapsed our housing where the Carmelite Missionaries Sister live. The roof fell in on us." She stopped and broke down in tears. "Four of my sisters in the room where I sleep died instantly. Like a horrible nightmare, I alone got out of the house. Then all of the houses in our village collapsed. Only one house is left standing." Sister Rosa buried her head in her hands. "All is lost. The Sisters who survived are in uncontrollable grief."

Fr. Stanley put his hand on Sister Rosa's shoulder and patted her gently. "We understand," he said. "And we are standing with you. Bless you, my dear." He turned around to the staff gathered around the young woman. "I think at this moment we must pray."

25

Any journey to Patzun had become almost impossible. Father Stanley, the two doctors and two nurses climbed over rocks and fallen trees that blocked the normal road. Parts of the dirt highway had broken through and tumbled down the steep cliff. Nevertheless, the team kept traveling with their supplies on their backs as well as bringing bundles with tents. Because the rigors of walking were familiar to all of them, they let nothing slow them down. By nightfall the team stumbled into the broken city.

Nurse Susan Andres suddenly stopped and gasped. "Look! The entire town has been wiped out like being hit in an incessant bombing."

Dr. Charles Harvey kept shaking his head. "There's not a building left standing."

They could see people struggling to walk down streets filled with debris. A few dogs looked disoriented and unsure of where to turn. People were lying in the streets. Children stared as the team approached. They seemed unsure whether these white-skinned new faces were friends or enemies.

"We must set up our tents," Fr. Stanley said. "Then we can get our operation going. Night will be falling soon, and it will be impossible to see in the dark. We brought those packets of dried soup. Once we get a fire going and water boiling, we can make a supper of some sort. I'm sure these people haven't eaten since the quake hit. We've got to keep moving fast."

People began coming out slowly to meet the team. Once they realized that Stanley's group brought medical care and goods, the villagers rushed toward them. Word spread quickly that they had medicine and bandages. Children surrounded the team and chattered away. The gloom began to break. Some of the villagers limped in and had to sit down immediately, but everyone began gathering around the fires and caldrons of boiling water. The aroma of cooking vegetable soup steaming up from the pot floated out. The scent of dried vegetables hadn't been diminished. People quickly gathered around the fireplace.

The fire provided illumination as night settled in. The people huddled around the glowing campfires as long as they could. Finally, the soup was gone, and the people returned to the remains of their houses. Against the backdrop of the moon's glow, the ruins of the village had war torn shadows with jagged pieces of blackness expressing nothing but brokenness. Still, if nothing else, Stanley's team had provided the first hot meal they had received in days.

***

Even before dawn broke, citizens were lined up for medical assistance. Fr. Stanley had already started fires to heat up other caldrons of soup. Everywhere he looked children were lining up for a piece of bread for breakfast. He felt someone pulling on his pant legs. Stanley looked down at a little boy who couldn't be much older than three-years. The little fellow had a distant faraway look in his eyes. Tears were still on his cheeks.

"*Utz a wach?*" Stanley asked in Tz'utujil

The boy's eyes widened in surprise. "*Utz.*"

Stanley picked him up. "Well, I've found a little friend." He carried him over to one of the small bowls hollowed out of a gourd that was sitting on a make-shift table. "Let's drink a little soup."

The child grabbed the gourd bowl and drank in large gulps, not stopping until the last drop was gone. When he finished, Stan wiped his mouth with a small cloth lying on the table. He sat the child on the ground, but the boy kept holding on to his leg. Other children gathered around. Dropping to his knees, he tried talking to them. Most didn't seem to know what happened to their parents. Probably their lost families were now buried under the debris of their former houses.

Still smiling at the children, Fr. Stanley pulled away and started walking toward the destroyed village. A smell had begun to fowl the air. No telling what lay below the rubble. It would take weeks, months, to begin to reconstruct the town. He kept walking, looking, feeling more depressed by the sight of destruction. Even the small village church had been smashed.

Off in the distance, Stanley heard the sound of an unexpected noise. The humming of a motor grew louder. He shielded his eyes and looked to the sky. Far away he could see three odd shapes flying toward the village. When Stanley looked again, he realized they were helicopters. U.S. Army helicopters! He wanted to shout for joy. They were coming to the village. He turned and ran back to the clearing at the edge of Patzun.

"Everybody stand back!" Fr. Stanley shouted. "Everyone get out of the way. Helicopters need space to land. Keep back!" He pointed to the sky

The villagers looked up and then began backing away. Some looked like they were seeing a mystical vision from the ancients. A few knew what they were seeing. Everyone cleared away. Slowly, the three choppers descended. Dust and broken tree limbs flew in all directions. The huge blades stopped swirling and the side doors opened. Military men jumped.

Standing head and shoulders above the crowd of Indians, Stanley waved and motioned for the soldiers to come to him.

"I'm Lieutenant Dan Beck" The leader saluted. "Are you in charge?"

"We walked in from Santiago Atitlan. I've got two doctors that are already working on the desperate. Two nurses also. Nobody's in charge. We're just trying to help."

"Good," Beck said with military precision. "If you've got people in critical condition, we can take them immediately back to Guatemala City."

"Excellent. Our doctors are working in that big tent over there." Fr. Stanley pointed over his shoulder. "We can find out in a hurry if we've got people to be transported."

The team of ten soldiers began to fan out across the village. Help was coming quickly. The military men seemed to know immediately what needed to be done. Services were rendered wherever required. The villagers stood in awe at the speed at which relief was coming.

"Sir!" A soldier rushed up to Lt. Beck. "I think we've got about fifteen people who need to be taken out of here as quickly as possible. They are ready to be loaded."

"Good," Beck said. "Get them in the helicopters."

Fr. Stanley said. "Lieutenant, we are grateful."

"We are grateful *to you,*" he answered. "You walked in when there were no roads and brought immediate help. I'm afraid there are many dead under that debris."

Stanley shook his head. "Afraid so. Do you have any idea about how bad the damage is across the country?"

"We're still calculating, but an educated guess is that we have around 26,000 deaths and maybe at least 80,000 injured. Over a million have been left homeless. The earthquake was simply catastrophic. The American military continues to fly in food, blankets, medicines, everything needed. It's a real task, but we won't quite until these people are taken care of."

"Wonderful," Fr. Stanley said. "The doctors and nurses we brought in will stay here as long as we are needed. I hope we can help rebuild this village."

Lt. Beck saluted. "Good luck, Father. Keep up the good work."

"We run on a different energy than luck," Stanley chuckled to himself and watched the soldier disappear into the helicopter. In a few minutes they were gone. At the least, the most critically injured were now on their way to care.

One of the nurses came out of the medical tent. Susan Andres looked worn. "You look a little tired," she said to the priest.

"All in a day's work," Stanley answered. "You don't exactly look like you're ready to dance yourself."

"That trek in was some walk," she said. "We carried in quite a load. Worth it though. We're doing plenty of good."

"I certainly hope so."

Susan Anders looked at him with a critical eye. "I've not known many men like you. You're a religious man, but you've come in here and started whipping things together. The children flock around you. You stop and talk to everyone like they are old friends. Stanley, old boy, you are a real pillar of hope in this devastated world."

26

Change drifted through the air. The rebuilding of houses, roads, churches kept everyone, every town, every village busy. The people responded energetically, but the tasks seemed nearly overwhelming. Nevertheless, the work went on without a hitch. An equally important change was coming to the MICATOKLA mission. Pope Paul VI had appointed Archbishop Quinn to lead the Archdiocese of San Francisco. A new Archbishop was coming to Oklahoma. Archbishop Charles A. Salatka was sent down from Michigan and was now presiding. While the new leader knew little about the Guatemala mission in particular, he understood well why it was important and wanted to give Father Rother's ministry his full support, Change would continue.

Taking care of repairs kept the entire mission staff working from early dawn into the late evening. The usual needs of the people had to be worked in while attending to the changes. Some of the issues brought special problems. One afternoon Fr. Stanley faced one of these significant changes while working from a tall ladder.

"Padre Francisco!" The short little man called up to the priest who was working on the side of the bell tower where a crack had opened. "Padre Francisco!" He waved his broad-brimmed cowboy style hat. "We must talk with you. My wife is here with me."

Fr. Stanley looked down. "Just a moment. I'll crawl down." He quickly scampered down the rungs. "What can I do for you?"

The man's wife stood with her head down. As usual, she wore a checkered, hand-woven poncho wrapped completely around her body and over the top of her head. From the bulge under the covering, Stanley could see she was carrying something.

"We have a problem," the man began and turned to his wife. She kept looking at the ground. "My wife just had a baby … two of them. We are poor people and cannot care for two babies at the same time." He shrugged. "Whether we like it or not, one of them must go to someone else. We want to give you the baby to take care of." The man turned to his wife. "Show him."

The woman pushed the poncho open. Wrapped in a small blanket, a four-pound baby girl began to stretch. One tiny arm reached above her thick head of black hair as she yawned. Her petite face still had closed eyes, but the baby's skin was beautiful, flawless brown."

"We call her Maria," the mother said so quietly that she could hardly be heard. "We are so sorry, but we don't have enough food … enough for all of us."

Stanley looked at the tiny baby. "A precious child," he said. "Certainly, we will find a right and good place for this little one. We will take good care of her."

"Gracias, gracias," the father said and kept shaking his hat and bowing up and down. "*Gracias, muchas gracias.*"

The mother bent down and kissed the baby before handing her to the priest. "Goodbye, Maria."

The father and mother turned and started walking away. Fr. Stanley watched them disappear down the street and then carried the little one back to the rectory. He carefully wrapped the little blanket around the tiny body.

"What ya' got there?" Susan Andres asked when he walked into the dining hall.

"A baby."

"Baby!" the nurse rushed over. "You're kidding!"

Fr. Stanley carefully laid Maria on the long dining room table. "Beautiful child. Her family couldn't keep her so they gave me the baby. We've got to find her a home."

Susan Andres peeked under the blanket. "Oh, my. A beautiful child indeed. What are you going to do?

"I guess I'll be getting up in the middle of the night to mix formula," Stanley said. "We certainly have a new member of the mission team."

"Can you find her a home?"

Stanley shrugged. "Somewhere. Somehow."

***

In the weeks that followed, baby Maria became a child of the mission. Stanley continued getting up at night to feed the tiny baby, but his diligence paid off as she steadily gained weight. Four pounds became six and her black hair never stopped growing. The Sisters attended her during the day. Surely baby Maria sensed she was adored.

In July, Jude Pansini returned to the mission with his wife. Years before he had been a priest, but now was married. The couple came for a Fiesta in honor of St. James, the patron of the parish. Natives wore their best costumes and danced in the streets. The horrors of the earthquake were pushed out of sight as the people celebrated for the first time in months.

"What do you think?" Fr. Stanley asked Jude while they strolled through Santiago Atitlan.

"I am amazed at what you have accomplished. Never have I seen the people so happy. Really warms my heart."

"We've all struggled rebuilding here and in the towns around us. The people were a major part of rebuilding houses and buildings. Of course, we were more fortunate here because the church wasn't significantly damaged. Towns like Patzun and Chimaltenango were smashed. Been a rough job getting those people back to normal. We had so, so many deaths."

Jude nodded. "I think I'll stop and buy one of those *frios crenas.*" He signaled to the vendor and held out some coins." The smell of frying tortillas from a nearby taco stand filled the air.

"*Gracias.*" The owner of the small ice cream cart answered. "*Muchas gracias, Senor.*"

In the middle of the zocalo, the center of the town, women were swirling around in their bright colored long dresses that spread waves of red, yellow, blue around the square. A few vendors had found balloons somewhere and were passing them out to the children.

You've been married a while," Fr. Stanley observed. "You must be a happy man."

"I am. My wife is a wonderful companion. I always got a little lonely, but now that's all gone.

"I notice you don't have any children."

Jude nodded.

"I can take care of that problem for you," Fr. Stanley said.

"What?" Jude Pansini frowned.

"I have a baby girl who needs a good home. How would you like to adopt baby Maria?"

The man's jaw dropped. "You're serious?"

Fr. Stanley nodded his head. "Absolutely."

"My wife would be ecstatic! How wonderful."

"I thought you'd like the idea. We will send you home with a delightful surprise."

***

Shortly after Jude and his family left with their new baby daughter, Stanley made a trip to Guatemala City to pick up supplies. After loading up, he met an old friend at an outdoor café. Father Ron Curtin ran a mission in the center of the city. Coming from Seattle, Washington, the priest had been in the country for several decades.

"You'll like this local beer, I think," Fr. Curtin said and handed him a bottle.

Stanley took a drink. "Not bad. A little heavy."

Fr. Ron smiled. "You ought to come to town more often. You're way out there in the countryside among the trees and bushes."

"We stay so busy that I'm almost completely absorbed with our mission. We've been helping rebuild some of the surrounding villages."

Fr. Ron nodded. "Have you noticed anything?"

"What do you mean?"

"Thousands of people died in that earthquake and countless numbers were injured. Who took care of them?"

"Well," Stanley thought for a moment. "We responded to those around us. Our mission took primary responsibility in many instances."

"Hmm," the priest leaned forward. "Any helicopters come in? And where were they from?"

"We have some American Army choppers carry the seriously injured out."

"And did you see any military response from the Guatemalan government?"

Fr. Stanley frowned. "What are you driving at?"

Fr. Ron leaned closer, speaking softly. "A great deal of discontent is building because the government did so little. Thousands died in virtually unmarked graves. Just dumped in. The people out in the villages are starting to question the actions of their own government. Groups of insurgents are beginning to form."

For a moment, Fr. Stanley looked around to make sure no one was listening. "Are you suggesting that a revolt is forming?"

"I'm telling you that tension is building across this country. The government is primarily a dictatorship run by the military. The natives are beginning to figure out that they are pawns, and the leadership of this country doesn't really care about them. That's a formula for big trouble."

"I've heard none of this," Fr. Stanley said.

"I didn't think so. You are a hard-working priest who takes care of the people. You don't get caught up in the country's politics. Nothing wrong with that, but the day is coming when we are going to get swept up in a struggle. Rebels will begin to emerge. The unnamed army will have guns. I just want you to be aware, Stan. In the coming months, I believe we are going to be facing danger."

Stanley blinked several times and wiped his forehead. "Are you certain about what you are saying?"

"I am afraid so. *Big* change is coming."

27

The work of the mission never stopped. Fr. Stanley continued making repairs to the church that reached back behind the 1976 earthquake. Another earthquake in 1960 had left its imprint on the church. Because the parish church of St. James the Apostles had been built centuries earlier, deterioration was inevitable. The retablo background behind the altar needed serious work. The piece stood nearly 20 feet high and had been cracked by the shaking. Repairs had to be done where pieces of wood had broken off. Stained glass windows were being installed and that took time. Having grown up with statues and religious images in the Okarche Holy Trinity Church, he knew how significant they could be. The task kept him working until late in the evening.

In the early morning, two expert woodcarvers had come to help. The priest met them at the door.

"Diego, you and your brother Nicolas have an excellent reputation," Stanley said.

"Ah, Padre Francisco, you honor the Chavez family. We are pleased to assist you."

"You know how to remove the grime from the retablo and rebuild the pieces of wood that have broken off. The same is true for the altar. Probably no one has worked at this task for centuries."

"*Si,*" Diego Chavez said. "We will treat every detail with the greatest respect."

"I would also like you to work into the retablo scenes from the Tz'utuijil culture wherever material must be added. Pictures of the people working, prayers. That sort of thing."

The Indians eyes opened wide. "Oh! Magnificent indeed. We always considered the altarpiece to be a living thing endowed with a *k'u'x,* a heart. Because the wood was placed there by our Mayan ancestors long ago, we believe it has spiritual life. We will handle everything with reverence. We will do our best."

Fr. Stanley smiled. "I know you will." He walked away thinking that he had struck another blow against the *cojfrias* control of the past and their beliefs. "Yes, indeed."

"Father!" a man's voice echoed from the rectory. "Father Francisco! We need your help!"

Antonio Ratzan and Juan Mendoza had been translating the three-year cycle liturgical lexionary for Sunday Mass into the Tz'utuijil language. By the 1970's a 200-page Spanish-Tz'utuijil prayer book had been developed for Santiago Atitlan as well as work had been done on translating the New Testament into the native language. Classes had been developed to teach the natives to read and write in their own language. The mission had developed literary instruction for the first time in Mayan history.

"What can I do for you boys?" Stanley asked.

"There are some English words that we don't understand," Antonio said. "You must help us make sense out of these phrases."

"Certainly." Fr. Stanley threw his arm over the man's shoulder. "You and Juan follow me."

"I don't understand this word Capernaum. Is Capernaum a drink?"

Stanley laughed. "No, no. Capernaum is town where Jesus started his ministry around the Sea of Galilee."

"Oh, no wonder we didn't get it," Antonio said.

As the day came to an end and supper was finished, Fr. Francisco pulled his usual chair close to the recorder that played liturgical and classical music. He leaned back in the chair and closed his eyes. Mozart's Requiem Mass filled his ears with the magnificent sounds of harmony and tranquility. Stanley relaxed.

"What's a farm boy doing listening to high-brow music?" Susan Andres interrupted the music.

Fr. Stanley jumped slightly, and his eyes popped open. "What?"

"I had no idea your taste in music was so excellent," she said.

"Don't ever underestimate farmers," he answered. "We are the jack of all trades."

"I'll be leaving tomorrow. My volunteer time is over. You've been the most interesting man to know."

"Well, Susan, we will always remember what you have contributed to this mission. It's been a pleasure having you here."

"I know you keep your nose to the grindstone, but I think you should be aware of the rumbles going on throughout South America." She handed him a copy of *Time* magazine. "You should read the articles about the unrest in Central America. The Church is being made the scapegoat by some of the governments that mistreated the natives. The stories suggest that terrible trials could be ahead."

"That's the second warning I've heard in recent days. I guess I better pay attention. Sounds like the pot is boiling."

"Father Stanley, you are surrounded by people who love and appreciate you. You've given so much to them, but don't let that blind you to what's on the other side of the mountain. These governments that are run by dictators and the military have proven to be vicious when challenged. Hard days could be ahead."

The priest sat up in his chair. "Thank you, Sister. I'll check this out."

***

Two weeks later, Fr. Stanley drove his Ford pick-up back to Guatemala City. He had called ahead to meet his friend Fr. Ron Curtain in the same street café where they talked last time. As usual, the streets were filled with traffic, but he noticed that there seemed to be more military trucks coming and going by. The afternoon sunlight felt warm and pleasant. No one paid him much attention as he sat along at the small round table.

"Ah! There you are." Father Curtain hurried up the sidewalk. "You were so intrigued by our glorious city and the bottle of beer I gave you, that you just had to hurry back."

"Not quite." Stanley grinned. "But I do want to follow up on our last conversation. You hinted that I hid out in the trees and didn't pay attention to politics. Well, but there was some truth in the fact that I do live in a remote village."

Fr. Ron smiled. "Maybe something I said did some good."

"I've been catching up on information about the unrest in the South and Central American countries. Apparently, there really are insurgents working on the people to rebel. Communist guerillas are reported to be out there plotting in the jungle. Is that what you were talking about?"

Ron Curtain pulled his chair up to the table and leaned closer to Stanley. "Here in the city, we naturally get the news every day. We can even tune in American channels. You've got to listen to me carefully, old friend. Yes, there is a serious uprising afoot and government will try to stamp it out at all costs."

"But the church has done nothing but try to help the people."

"That's the bind. These despotic governments trust no one and they are suspicious of the help we give the people. They suspect that their citizens may be more loyal to us than the government."

"Are you saying that we are caught in the middle?"

"Exactly. The more good we do, the more the politicians hate us."

For a long time, Stanley said nothing. The two men silently looked at each other. Finally, Fr. Stanley asked, "Can you give me any examples of brutality?"

"There was a massacre in the Northern part of this country. At the last count 115 men and women as well as children were slaughtered. Of course, the government suppressed the story. Most recently, we had a social activist priest who focused on the problems of the downtrodden. They caught him on the outskirts of the city, and he was machine gunned down. Of course, nobody seemed to know who did it."

Fr. Stanley rubbed his mouth nervously. "God help us."

"Here's another one to think about. We had a priest who worked with the Maryknoll Fathers. He had started working with the miners to develop a union. If he could get the union organized, they would begin to have leverage with the government for better pay for the workers." Fr. Ron leaned even closer and spoke more softly. "Last week, the priest was shot down. None of it was reported."

"You live with these stories?

"Every day.

Stanley shook his head, barely able to grasp what he was hearing.

"Now here's the final story for you," Fr. Ron said. "The land is owned by a small number of people while millions of Indians struggle to survive and have nothing. All the sugar, corn, and beef is used to compete with America. So, the government sees the existence of Indians as a problem. They've come up with a solution. Kill off the males and have their wives impregnated by non-Indians so they can improve the race with fresh Spanish blood. Just get rid of the natives by pushing them into non-existence. How do you like that idea?"

Another truck load of soldiers zoomed down the street. Cars immediately got out of their way. People seemed to walk faster down the street.

"I don't know how we can get prepared for this threat." Stanley said.

Fr. Ron shook his head. "That's just it. You can't."

28

May 1979

Two weeks passed quickly. Improvement on the Church of Saint James the Apostle continued with Diego and Nicolas Chavez showing up early each day to apply their wood carving skills to the altar and retablo. Because of their craftsmanship, the work went well. The Chavez brothers took a particular delight in helping the church. When Fr. Stanley walked in, they laid their tools down and waved to him.

"Ah, Padre Francisco," Diego called out. "What do you think?"

For a moment, the priest walked back and forth studying the twenty-feet high retablo carefully. "Most excellent," he said. "You are doing a beautiful job."

Diego and Nicolas grinned. "Thank you, Padre." The brothers climbed down their ladders. "I think we are making good progress. As you suggested, we carved in a figure kneeling in prayer beside corn stalks. I think the people will like this addition."

"I trust so. When do you boys think you will be finished?"

Diego looked around and then walked closer to Fr. Stanley. "We are concerned that trouble is coming," he said softly. I'm not sure we should stay here in Santiago Atitlan much longer."

"What do you mean?"

"Did you see the letter? Diego whispered.

Fr. Stanley frowned. "Letter? No."

"An anonymous letter has been circulating among the people threatening action against what they call 'the enemies of the people.' The names of important people are listed, the mayor, teachers, mission staff. I know Father Adan has just arrived to work here, but his name was included."

The priest took a deep breath. "And my name?"

"On the list of targets, you are number eight and Father Adan is number nine."

"Look!" Fr. Stanley placed his hand on Diego's shoulder. "Someone is simply trying to frighten the people. I don't know if it's the army or the insurgents or some nut case, but they want to scare the people. We must not yield to that influence. We must tell everyone to ignore this letter."

"People are worried," Diego said. "We don't want to get swept up in some sort of confrontation."

"Good. Just keep working and tell all your friends to ignore these threats."

Diego shrugged. "I-I don't know. Some of the local citizens are talking about leaving."

"Where will they go?" Stanley pressed. "If a rebellion is taking shape, the entire country will be caught up in the struggle. They are safer here."

"I know, I know." Diego shrugged. "I just thought you should be informed."

"Thank you. I'll look into the matter. Now, let's get back to work."

Diego nodded and started back up the ladder. He turned and gave a half-hearted smile. "I hope you are right."

Fr. Rother walked out of the church, thinking about what he had heard. Perhaps he had not taken the situation seriously enough. Obviously, he needed to know more about the turmoil unfolding in his own backyard. Who sent out such a threatening letter? The insurgents? The government? Someone local? What are the facts behind this story? He needed to talk with someone who was better informed. Had to be a person beyond the local community. Fr. Stanley knew of only one person. Fr. Ron Curtain.

***

"Fr. Ron? It's been an experience getting a call through to you. The phone lines being what they are and then running you down in Guatemala City took half a day."

"Stan. You still out there in the jungle?"

Fr. Stanley laughed. "Wouldn't call it the bush country, but I'm here in Santiago Atitlan at the mission. We've had a strange incident that I need to talk with you about. A threatening letter has been circulated through the town. Whoever sent it, is suggesting assassinations of prominent citizens. The death list has my name as well as my associates. I made number 8."

There was a long pause. "Listen to me carefully and don't say anything else. Your phone line could have been bugged. Mine too. Much has happened since we last talked. No telling who might be listening. I'm not going to say anymore, but I will come and talk with you in person. To avoid detection, I'm not going to say when I'll be there. Just watch for me."

For several moments, Stanley said nothing. Finally, he answered. "I-I see. Okay. I'll look for you."

The phone went dead. Fr. Stanley hung up slowly. Matters were indeed more serious than he'd thought.

Father Stanley had not taken long to obtain a copy of the letter. Throughout the day, he thought about how turmoil might affect the mission. The facts that Diego Chavez told him were true. He and Father Adan were listed as prime targets. Much, much more than he would have guessed was going on.

The day unfolded as usual. Locals dropped in to talk about their problems. Unexpected situations arose. Staff members sought his guidance. Two of the Sisters needed his help. He had little time to think about the letter. Still, the priest noticed many of the indigenous villages seemed more tense and nervous than usual. At 4:30 in the afternoon, an old blue Chevrolet pulled up in front of the rectory. Fr. Ron Curtain had wasted no time in getting there. He got out of the car.

"You didn't let the dust settle in getting here." Stanley stood on the front porch. "That car of yours took these back roads rather well."

Fr. Curtain started walking up the stairs. "Got to be resourceful out here in the boon docks." He laughed. "Just like you do night and day."

"Come on in, Ron. Got a cup of coffee waiting for you."

They walked in and sat down on one of the long dinner table benches. "I'm afraid the coffee's been sitting there all day," Stanley said. "Might be a little stale."

"I'll pass. We need to talk quickly so I can get back to the city. I must bring you fully up to date."

"Can you give me a history of some sort about what's created this upheaval?"

"You know about the fact that the largest percent of the land has always been controlled by a small group that go clear back to the original control by the Spanish. Of course, some American owned companies are part of that domination that has left the natives out in the cold. That's where the problem started. The original poor Mayan Indians had to struggle to survive."

"Yes, we've seen that problem. I know well about the poverty of the people."

"A United States backed coup d'état in 1954 brought the regime of Carlos Castittlo Armas to power. This started a series of right-wing military dictators. In 1960, a left-wing revolt against General Fuentes kicked off the current explosions. Out in the hinterlands, a group now known as MR-13 began to form. Social discontent began to surface among the natives. Many of these Indians organized into their own secret groups. They started clandestine attacks on the government troops. Much of this rebellion went unreported, but tension was building like a runaway steam roller careening down the mountainside."

"While I'm working out here with my people, all this chaos had been unfolding?"

The Making of a Martyr

"All over the country!" Fr. Curtain shrugged. "The problems have been rumbling out in the bushes, but the opposition has been getting organized. The insurgents are now operating at a new level. At the same time, the Guatemalan military has been attempting to eliminate all of the government's enemies. Sometimes they operate in the open and sometimes they shoot people in the alley. Right now, they are fighting to control the society at every level. When the top dogs look at the church, they're not sure which side we're on. Consequently, they kill our people and leaders to make sure no problems emerge. People just disappear."

Fr. Stanley thought for a moment. "How strong are these insurgents?"

"Depends. There are a number of groups. Some are more dangerous than others."

"Are these guerillas after us?" Stanley asked.

Fr. Curtain shook his head. "Our basic concern is the government military. Military intelligence plans the strikes and assassinations. The so-called disappearances are generally organized by them. Thousands are being killed while many, many good people simply disappear. Because the insurgency is strongest in the rural areas, government repression sometimes wiped-out entire villages. You don't hear about it because the government controls communications. That's why it's dangerous to discuss any of this on the telephone."

"But all we've done is help the poor, the dispossessed, the Indians," Fr. Stanley protested. "Our concern has been to help them live better lives. Everyone knows that's been our only task."

"Look, Stan. The military has gone after people who are academics, trade unionists, journalists, and even street children. They want to consolidate their grip on the country. My sources of information tell me that they are also particularly after the Mayan people. Your best hope is to get out of the country.

"Listen, Ron. The Mayans have become my people. I'm not going to abandon them."

"Then you may have to face the consequences."

29

May 1980

"Father Stanley!" Sounded like Father Adan calling from the front porch of the rectory.

Stan looked up from playing with some of the village children where he had been in some sort of game. He was now the "it" with the children running to keep him from catching them. "Father Stanley! You've got visitors."

"Okay." The priest ended the chase by tagging one of the children and trotted back to the rectory. "What's going on?"

Father Adan motioned over his shoulder. "You've got some nuns inside waiting to talk with you."

"Really? I wasn't expecting anyone."

"Well, they just dropped in to see you."

Father Stanley shrugged. "Let's see what they want."

Father Adan led the way up the stairs of the rectory. Now Fr. Rother's right-hand man, he always took care of the details. Father Adan had proved to be an excellent associate.

They walked into the large dining hall with the smell of lunch still lingering in the air. Four sisters immediately stood. Two had on the formal habits of the Carmelites and the other two were more casually dressed. They all made a slight bow before sitting down.

"My goodness, Sisters. I had not anticipated your coming. We would have made some nice cake and a little wine prepared for you. Unfortunately, we have no cake on hand."

"Thank you, Reverend Father." The leader of the group spoke. "I am Sister Elizabeth. My comrades are Sisters Angelica, Maria, and Joann. We are actually from two different communities. Sister Angelica and myself are Carmelites of St. Theresa. My friends are professed Sisters from different Mayan groups."

"Interesting," Fr. Stanley said. "I don't think I've heard of sisters joining together from such different backgrounds. News to me. Excellent."

"Our allegiance to one another is new almost to everyone," Sister Elizbeth said. "We learned that supporting Mayan amalgamations is important to you, Father. That is why we have come. We are blending our cultures as we serve the Lord."

"Important," Fr. Stanley said. "Most interesting."

"We have come to ask you to serve with us in the Santiago Apostol Parish. We were impressed with your service after the earthquake. We believe you could carry our work forward."

"My goodness," Fr. Stanley smiled. "I am honored by such a request. I'll have to give it some thought. We have much to do here. Right now, we are making important renovations to our village church. Work is being done on the retablo as well as the entire sanctuary. I will take a hard look at our schedule and let you know in a few days. I suppose you want me mainly to celebrate Mass for your convent and community."

"Yes," Sister Elizabeth said. "Our Sisters work in the village in literacy, catechism, liturgical music, as well as working directly with the girls and women of the parish. Of course, we also care for the sick."

"Naturally," Fr. Stanley answered. "Please give me several days and I'll be back in touch."

The four Sisters stood and smiled. "We thank you for your time," Sister Angelica added. "We will all be hoping and waiting for your response."

Fr. Stanley watched the Sisters disappear through the front door. Their visit was important, and he could see new possibilities opening. Maybe he would come to know these comrades in the faith much better.

From the opposite end of the dining hall, Father Adan reappeared. "This is your day for unexpected visitors. While you were talking with the Sisters, another man came. You already know Father Ron Curtain."

"Father Ron! He was here only a short time ago. I wonder what's developed?"

The younger priest broke into the room with long, bold strides. "Always nice to come out here to the 'jungle' for a few laughs," Curtain said. "Need to periodically check on you to make sure you're doing something besides sleeping on the job."

"You have some kind of sense of humor," Stanley answered. "However, if my experience serves me right, you have something more on your mind that coming out here in the country for a breath of fresh air."

"What a psychic! You read my mind as if it were an open book."

"Yeah, a book with a few pages missing. Sit down and rest your feet. The coffee pot is still on today. Now I can offer you a nice hot coffee. Of course, I can always produce a little glass of wine... red or white."

"Your hospitality exceeds my expectations. "I would take a little red to parch my poor dry throat."

Fr. Stanley walked over to a cabinet and took out a bottle of cabernet. He poured two glasses and took one to Fr. Ron Curtain. "I think you'll like this."

The priest took a sip. "Not bad. Now, my friend, we must get down to business. Serious business."

Stanley frowned. "Oh?"

Fr. Ron's face changed. The smile disappeared. His eyes became intense, penetrating, hard, "I want you to listen to me carefully. When I was here last, I shared with you the chaos exploding across the country. Priests and workers being killed. You listened but I don't think my warnings sunk in very deeply."

"I wouldn't say that, Ron. Of course, I took you seriously."

"Stan, your interest is totally with these people. You serve them remarkably well. They love and respect you. I know that you were concerned when they put your name on a list for assassination, but you tended to believe it was about someone else. Listen to me carefully. It's not."

Stanley rubbed his cheek and blinked several times. "Something more is going on?" he finally said.

"Yes! The soldiers are moving toward your village. You know a number of people have already left. When they get here, your life isn't worth a plug nickel. You'll move to the top of their list of who gets knocked off."

"I believe the villagers will protect me."

"The villagers?" Ron scoffed. "With their military rifles, the soldiers will kill the Indians as easily as hunting rabbits. You're just one more target. It's that simple."

Fr. Stanley kept rubbing his cheek. For nearly a minute he said nothing. Finally, he said, "There is an urgency in your voice. What do you want me to do?"

"Listen to me carefully," he repeated the same words he had already said a number of times. "I want you to leave with me right now. Make up any excuse you wish. Tell your associate to take over the work. Go out and get in the car with me and leave this minute. An airplane ticket will be waiting for you at the airport."

Stan stared at his friend. Fr. Ron meant every word. Never had he seen such an intensity in a man's eyes. The starkness of his demand scared Stan. There was no voiding the implications.

Fr. Ron's entire stiff posture made Stan feel like the assassins were already at the door. Who knows who they might kill first? Himself?

"We don't have much time left." Ron pointed over his shoulder toward his car. "Got to go now!"

"My sister's anniversary of twenty-five years with the order of the Adorers of the blood of Christ is coming up. I could say that I am going back for the commemoration and that I would return to celebrate with the family."

"That's an excellent reason. Tell Father Adan where you're going and to take cover. He's local and will know what to do. Now let's get out of here. The clock is ticking."

Stanley rushed out of the room. He met his associate on the stairway and had a brief conversation with Fr. Adan, Stan grabbed a bag and hurried back down the stairs. When he walked out the front door of the rectory, he could hear Curtain's car already running. "There's real urgency to what we are doing?"

"Stan, more that you realize. Believe me."

30

The old black Chevrolet Fr. Ron Curtain had picked up in the city swirled to a stop in front of the La Aurora Airport serving Guatemala City. Actually, six kilometers from the downtown in the small town of Finta San Isidro, the terminal had several soldiers standing around with carbines and machine guns at their sides. Traffic coming into the airport had proved much better than the congestion in the heart of the capital city. Still, soldiers could be seen everywhere. The Chevrolet pulled into a parking space.

"I noticed we changed vehicles in the city," Fr. Stanley said. "Do you always do that?"

Curtain shrugged. "Let's call it an adjustment for the times."

"You're just full of these little 'adjustments' as you call them. Ron, you know a lot more than you are saying."

"Don't we all."

"No, not these kinds of shifts. You've convinced me that I'm living in dangerous circumstances. Maybe you can be a bit more candid."

"Someday over a nice glass of wine, I'll be more explicit, but not at this moment. Our task is to get you on that airplane and out of here."

"Ron, your insights are far more reaching than reading a newspaper and listening to gossip. You don't pick up this information from casual conversations. You seemed to know that I had to immediately get out of my village. Level with me. How did you know?"

"Stan, I can't tell you anymore than I have. Obviously, you understand that I know what I'm talking about. That's all that counts. Now let me give you one final suggestion. You're wearing that homemade jacket that came straight out of your village and makes you look like a Tz'utujil, or however you say it, a sympathizer. I'd suggest you put it in your bag before you get out of the Jeep. You won't be so noticeable except you're ten feet tall."

Fr. Stanley nodded and began taking the coat off.

"I already have your ticket." Fr. Curtain pulled a packet out of his shirt. "Along with your passport, this will get you through."

"You already have my ticket?" Stanley blinked several times. "How'd you know I'd go?"

Fr. Curtain said with no emotion, "I figured it'd be you in a seat or a wooden box."

Stanley froze. "You're kidding!"

"I don't kid about these matters. Don't come back until they have changed the government. Goodbye, Stan."

The priest slowly stepped out of the battered old chevy with his bag to his side. "How can I ever thank you?" Fr. Stanley choked and could barely speak. "Th-thanks."

"By staying alive." Fr. Curtain waved. "God's best to you." The car pulled away and back into the line of traffic.

Fr. Stanley watched him disappear out of the terminal. He slowly turned toward the entrance and walked past the soldiers. His nearly six-foot height made him tower above the guards. As Stanley walked past, they glowered, but did nothing. He walked into the small terminal with no hesitation in his stride.

***

"Something to drink?"

Stanley jumped. For a moment he wasn't sure where he was. The woman bending over in front of him looked totally unknown. He looked a second time and realized he was on an airplane. "Ah-ah, no thanks," She moved on.

It took several moments to get awake. He looked around the airplane and the sparsely filled commercial flight. Probably not many people were coming and going with the political upheaval in the country. For the first time since Fr. Curtain had rushed him out of Santiago Atitlan, did he really have time to reflect. In retrospect, he felt like he had been swept out the door in a whirlwind of danger. With the steady hum of the airplane's engines in the background giving him consolation, he could think.

In truth, Fr. Ron's assault on his reasoning and had sent him running. Now the fact that he had left bothered him. Everything had been so sudden, but was that the right response? He doubted it. No question that Curtain knew what he was talking about, but something didn't feel right.

Growing up as a farm boy, Stanley had been used to the orderly procession of each day's chores. They got up early and took care of the chickens and animals. Everyone had an assignment they did well. No one listened to the news more than the weather report.

They just went about their business. As the day unfolded, little attention was paid to politics. Oh, yes, they voted but no one thought about violence or uprisings. In high school, his interest had been in F.F.A and what additional information he learned about farming. In retrospect, Stan realized how smooth everything had been.

During his struggles in seminary, he dealt with his conflicts by praying. In fact, even when he was sure he was going to fail, intercession had carried him through. The idea of a physical assault never entered his mind. Daily Mass had inspired him to continue. Even during the difficult days at St. John's seminary in San Antonio, the power of his devotion had made the difference. Never would he have considered himself in physical danger.

The truth was that he wasn't really prepared to personally grasp what Fr. Ron Curtain told him in their first discussion time about upheavals in the country. He simply wasn't tuned in to be involved in political controversy. The idea of a personal threat had been way too distant to him. Even the idea that his name was on a death list had seemed more like a prank, a Halloween scare. Ron's second visit had cracked that shell. Naivete had been knocked out the window. He realized the possibility of confrontation and personal danger was real and immediate. Yes, Fr. Ron knew what he was talking about!

And where did this young priest get such profoundly deep insight? Fr. Ron had sources of some sort that fed him information meant to help the church and save the clergy. There had been desperate times in the past when the church had been in similar dire straits. Earlier in the century, Mexico had gone through a violent upheaval that put the church and clergy in danger. In 1917, a new Constitution was enacted that was hostile to the Church and religion. The result promulgated an anti-clericalism similar to that seen in France during the Revolution. Fr. Ron seemed to have penetrating insight from that past. A parallel situation was now unfolding in Guatemala, and he simply hadn't recognized how serious the signs were.

"A little something to drink?" the steward asked.

"Thank you," Fr. Stanley answered. "I'd take a little glass of red wine."

"Certainly," The woman handed him a small bottle and a glass. "Here's a snack to go with it." She laid a cellophane wrapped cookie on his tray.

Stanley took a sip and closed his eyes. He seemed to be living through a time warp that wasn't telling him anything new but resharpening his perception to the past. Political realities that he hadn't considered were opening up new insights that he had to face. All he had ever wanted to be was a humble parish priest, but this new situation demanded that he be politically astute. Insurgents were in a war to unseat the government and the natives were pawns in the fight. The Catholic Church had become the prime target and clergy the victims. Yes, Ron was right. They would kill him if they got the chance.

The steady roar of the airplane's engines again drowned out his thoughts. His realizations had left him tired and exhausted. His body had almost begun to ache from the impact of his discoveries. He closed his eyes and started drifting away. One thought lingered. The opposition would kill him if they got the chance.

31

The secretary rushed into the Bishop's office. "Sir, I just got a phone call from Gertrude Rother. She wanted you to know that Father Rother called from Dallas, Texas. He made a totally unexpected flight out of Guatemala. Father Rother asked her to call you so you'd know he's back. Apparently, the airplane is on the way right now.

Archbishop Salatka stiffened and nodded his head slowly. "This is not good. I've been worried about him for some time. He wouldn't have made an abrupt departure unless the situation had worsened."

"I understand there's some sort of revolution going on down there," the secretary said. "He might be caught up in that struggle."

"We've been getting bad reports from the region for some time. Bishops of other diocese across the country have talked with me about the problem. It's a serious matter."

"I knew you'd want to know immediately."

"Yes." Salatka stood up. "Please get my hat and overcoat. I want to be there when Father Stanley arrives. I want to welcome him back and give him my blessing. I am sure he'll appreciate a word of encouragement."

"Should I get the car? I know it's beginning to get cold outside. The weatherman said we could get snow today."

"Yes, have my car at the entrance. I'm on my way."

***

Franz and Gertrude Rother sat close to the large window watching airplanes taking off and landing. Time had made its mark on them, but Gertrude always was well-dressed. Today, they sat on the edge of their seats staring anxiously at the flight patterns. A light snow had begun to fall from a gray sky.

"Stan always lets us know well in advance when he is coming," Gertrude said. "Never has he called so unexpectedly and said he was already on his way."

Franz nodded slowly. "Never." He took a deep breath. "I'm afraid something's gone wrong. Don't hear much about it on the news, but maybe them peoples down there's gone haywire."

Gertrude could only shake her head. "Just don't know. Well, regardless I'm glad to have him coming home."

Archbishop Salatka came walking briskly down the hall. "Well, look who's here," Gertrude said. Both of the Rothers stood up. "Wonderful you could come, Archbishop."

"Friends, I'm so glad you called me. I wanted to be here to greet Father Stanley myself. Hope he is well."

"So kind of you to come," Gertrude Rother said. "I know Stanley will appreciate your being here very much.

"Wouldn't have it any other way," Bishop Salatka said.

"I think that's his plane." Franz Rother pointed toward the American Airlines planes coming in for a landing. He glanced at his watch. "Sure is right on time."

The parents and the bishop watched the airplane taxi to the terminal. A walkway was quickly pushed up next to the side of the airplane. Passengers immediately began filing out. The wind whipped their coats around them.

"There he is!" Gertrude cried out. "That's our boy."

Stanley only had on a lightweight jacket. He hurried down the steps and disappeared into the ground level of the terminal. Passengers had to climb the stairs to come out inside the terminal. Ten men walked in before Stanley walked out.

"Son!" Gertrude ran toward him and hugged him.

Franz followed with a hearty hug. The bishop stood behind him.

"Archbishop Salatka!" Stanley exclaimed.

"Welcome home, Father Rother," the bishop said. "It's wonderful to see you."

"What a surprise to see you here," Stanley said. "Such a blessing."

"I wanted to welcome you myself." The archbishop eyed him critically. "My boy, I think you've lost some weight. You look a little thinner. Aren't you freezing?"

"Well, it's not winter down there, and I had to leave quickly. All I have on are these worn jeans and this short sleeve blue shirt. I had to leave so suddenly that I left most of my clothes behind."

"Leave quickly?" Gertrude winced. "Something *was* wrong."

"Oh, I came back for Sister Marita's celebration of twenty-five years of her profession."

"But that was several weeks ago," Franz said.

"I thought we'd have a private celebration," Stanley joked.

"Just as I feared," the archbishop said. "Fr. Rother, after you've had some time to rest up, we must have a conversation as soon as possible."

"I'll look forward to talking," Fr. Stanley said.

"Call my office. I'll make time whenever it is convenient for you."

"Thank you. I'll call in the next day or so. I'll need to get acclimated first. Thank you so much for coming."

The three Rother's walked away with the son standing between his parents. The archbishop watched but didn't move.

"Stan's not telling the whole story," the Archbishop Salatka mumbled to himself. "Not at all. He's been in danger. No question about it."

The archbishop walked slowly out of the terminal with his mind churning. When he stepped outside, the wind slapped him in the face. The cold weather had definitely picked up. All the way back to his office, he kept thinking about what the entire story might be. He wanted to know the depth of the instability in Guatemala before he talked with Father Stanley. He certainly trusted Stan completely, but this priest had a way of presenting matters in the most positive light. More was needed. There was nothing positive about his leaving his clothes back in the rectory.

Archbishop walked in the building at a fast clip and barely slowed when he came to his secretary's desk. "I want you to call the State Department and find out who's on the desk for Guatemalan affairs. Get them on the line so I can talk with them. Tell them that the Archbishop of Oklahoma City is calling. Please do this as quickly as possible."

The archbishop continued on into his private office. Hanging up his hat, he sat down to think. The afternoon sunlight cast shadows across the room. A reflection from the large Crucifix drifted down the wall. For a long time, he stared at that shadow. From his many years in the Church, he had become apprehensive about what that form meant. All priests pledged to live their lives in fidelity to the Cross. Undoubtedly, they began by thinking of the meaning as symbolic, but if it became necessary, they understood it must be taken literally when such a time overwhelmed them. How well the Archbishop understood that paradox. The symbolism could also be literal. And now Father Stanley could be standing at the threshold of such a decision. Such an action was not only out of his reach, but it was inconceivable that he should come between any man and his calling. Every man had to make his own solitary decision alone. That was always the way of the Cross.

The door opened without a knock. "A gentleman named Allen McAvee is on the line," the secretary said. "He will talk with you."

The bishop picked up the phone. "Archbishop Salatka here. I have personnel working in Guatemala and need an update on their safety. Can you give me direct information?"

"Thank you for calling, sir. Yes, the American government has been following developments in this country for a number of years. We have observed the actions of men like dictator Jorge Unico, the actions of Jacob Arbenz, Arevalo, and so forth. Of course, we know about the actions of the United Fruit Company that has also had an effect on the country and the people. We continue to follow the uprising and civil war that is now unfolding."

"What about the safety of my personnel, my priests working in Guatemala?"

"I am sorry to tell you that the United States government cannot guarantee the safety of any citizen and that we have moved most of our personnel out of the country. The Roman Catholic Church is definitely under attack in that country. We would suggest that all citizens stay out of Guatemala."

Archbishop Salatka took a long, deep breath. "Thank you for your assistance. Your straightforward response is most helpful. Good day sir." He hung up the telephone.

For a long time, the archbishop stared at the crucifix. It certainly is not symbolic.

32

The Rother's pulled up in front of the white farmhouse where little had changed in over fifty years. Fr. Stanley got out of the car slowly and looked around. The flat, rolling farmland looked just as it always had. An old faded red tractor was still parked next to the barn. The few elm trees had grown taller and survived decades of the blistering summer heat, but everything else appeared remarkably the same. He walked up the front steps slowly. Of course, he had done so a thousand times but today that walk seemed from another lifetime. Everything was the same; everything was different. His life had taken unexpected turns and twists that changed his perspective on what was before him.

"Son," Franz said. "We've got something for you in the house. Come on in." He held the screen door open.

Stanley walked in. That familiar scent of the house settled around him. The wallpaper, the furniture . . . everything was what he expected. The realization reminded him how different his world in Santiago Atitlan was from what his wonderfully loving childhood home had been.

"We want you to sit down at the dining room table," Gertrude said. "Come over here."

Stanley slipped into a chair where he had eaten countless meals with his sister across the table and Jim and Tom on the other side. Of course, Jim was gone now, and his chair would always be empty.

"Son." Franz pointed toward the kitchen door. "Watch what you see." He clapped his hands.

A woman in a black habit popped through the door. "Surprise!"

Stanley's mouth dropped and he leaped to his feet. "Betty Mae!" He rushed over. "Can't believe my eyes. Here you are!"

She hugged him. "I think you're the only person in the world who still calls me Betty Mae."

"And I bet I'm about the only one of two brothers you've got left who know the truth."

"They tell me you came for my celebration that was only several weeks passed."

Stanley shrugged. "I am a bit late. We tell time differently in Guatemala. We don't measure it by hours but by months."

Sister Marita laughed. "Different indeed."

"Why don't the two of you sit on the front porch and talk," Franz said.

"Little cold for that," Sister Marita said. "Let me drive us into Okarche and show Stan the new restaurant. Built since he was here last. He'll enjoy a peek at the town."

"Sure," Franz said. "Here's the keys to the car. Have a good time."

They stepped out into the winter wind and quickly got in the car. Sister Marita swung the car t back on the road.

"I don't care what protocol says," Stanley said. "I'm going to call you Betty Mae regardless."

She laughed. "Stan, you're as big a tease as ever. I thought we ought to talk a bit before you speak with the folks. We know you didn't show up with only the clothes on your back by accident. The suddenness of your return has jarred our parents. I need to bring you up to date on how they are."

Stanley nodded and for a long time said nothing. They rode in silence.

"Look over there!" Betty Mae pointed to the new café. "That's now the hang-out where the kids gather. You'll like it best in the summer, but it'll do for today."

"Well, at least somethings have changed in this predictable little town."

She laughed and pulled up to the curb. "Come on in."

Stanley closed the car door behind them. Betty Mae walked up to the counter. "Two hot chocolates. please"

The waitress nodded. "Good to see you this morning, Sister Marita."

Stanley walked to a table in the back out of the way of people coming in. In this small town, he didn't expect many folks to walk in , but the chances were good they might know this unusual brother and sister religious team.

Betty Mae placed the cup in front of him. "Smells good, doesn't it?"

"What a nice surprise."

"Stan, you can tell our parents have aged. You can see it in their faces."

"Yes, I noticed it at the airport." He looked down for a moment. "They looked worried."

"Jim's death took a terrible toll on the entire family. We knew what was coming, but you never get prepared for death when it's in your own household. Dad went out into the fields alone and didn't come back for hours. I thought mom would never stop crying. We were always a close family, but even closer than I even realized."

Stan nodded. "I couldn't talk about Jim's passing with my colleagues. Took me a long time even to mention it to anyone."

Betty Mae nodded. "After we made some adjustments, our parents began to think even more intently about you. They were so proud when you went down there as a missionary, but they also recognized how different that world was. They tuned in to every bit of news they could get about Guatemala. They've become highly aware of the revolution going on in that country. Mom and dad worry all the time."

"I've been concerned about them," Stanley said. "I don't write much about the upheavals."

"They called me immediately when they discovered you were on your way. They knew something was up. On one hand, they were glad you were coming. On the other, they figured you were in trouble. Showing up with nothing but the clothes on your back confirmed it. They won't say much, but they are scared to death for you. Tell me the truth, Stan. Is the struggle that bad?"

"It is. Many priests have been murdered. The government has turned on the Church as an excuse for their problems. I left quickly because I had become a target."

Betty Mae's lips pursed. She could only nod.

"But I'm here now so nobody's chasing me down the streets of Okarche. We can relax."

"You always try to put the best face on everything, but I know the war will not change in the near future. Will you go back?"

Stanley rubbed his forehead. "Maybe I shouldn't have left in the first place. I can't say right now. I know I can't turn my back on my responsibilities, on my people. I guess I've got a great deal to think about."

Betty Mae frowned. "You must be cautious about what you tell mom and pop. Spare them any frightening details because they would worry and obsess endlessly.

Stan nodded.

Betty Mae didn't say anything more for several minutes. The brother and sister didn't look at each other for a long while. "I know the only thing that matters now is what God is calling you to do," she finally said.

"That's true" Stan said. "The question is what is the will of the heavenly Father."

33

As the cold of winter increased, the days seemed to drag by. Fr. Stanley knew that the archbishop would gladly appoint him to a parish in Oklahoma, but that didn't fit. He knew that a divine call had sent him to Santiago Atitlan and that couldn't be discounted. For hours, the priest stared down the hall in his parent's house and looked out the back door toward the field when wheat grew. The green winter shoots covered the fields and would begin to grow taller when warmer days came. But what of his calling? Could he just sit still? The long, deary days had become filled with agony. He felt on edge and misplaced.

"A special delivery letter came for you, Stan," Gertrude said. "I knew you'd want to read it immediately."

"Thank you," Stanley opened the envelope immediately.

Dear Fr. Rother,

I wanted to give some clarification as to why you departed the country so immediately. The military has been ruthless. They have really gone after the guerilla groups, killing them on sight. Murder, kidnapping, torture are the order of the day.

Three priests were murdered and another one kidnapped. The pastor of Chajul Father Jose Maria Gran Ciel had been ministering to his parish members when he was shot in the back while riding home on horseback. His sacristan Domingo Bats was also murdered.

You must keep these facts in mind as you look to the future.

Your friend and brother in Christ,

Father Ron Curtain

Stanley said nothing but folded the sheet of paper and put it back in the envelope. He stuffed the envelope in his pants pocket. Once again, he silently looked down the long hallway and through the door out into the wheat field.

"I'm going into town," Sister Marita came down the stairs and said, "Do you need anything?"

"No, don't think so. I was sitting here thinking. You know, I haven't heard from Sister Clarissa in quite a while. Do you know where she is?"

"Yes, she's been retired for some time. I think she is in St. Anne's retirement home in Oklahoma City."

"Really? Out there on the north side of the city? Not far from here?"

"Believe so."

"I think I'll borrow Dad's old pickup and run in to pay her a visit. Through the years she's been such an encouragement to me. Maybe I can offer her a little cheer."

"That's a nice thought. She'd be delighted to have you visit. I'll call and let her know you are coming." Sister Marita disappeared through the back door.

For a few moments, Stanley reflected on the sound advice she'd given him through hard times. The good Sister always had something important that helped him when everything had become obscure. A decision about whether to stay or go back to Guatemala remained constantly before his eyes. No one wanted him to return and yet he could not look away. Maybe today Sister Clarissa would have more important advice.

***

Franz Rother's red pickup turned into the driveway of St. Anne's and circled into the parking lot. The pristine retirement center carried a quietness that settled around him and the old truck. Fr. Stanley had worn a collar and knew that would please Sister Clarissa. He swung open the large glass door and walked through the breezeway into the lobby. Parked next to the front wall was a wheelchair and a smiling happy face.

"Sister Clarisa!"

"Well, well, here's my fifth-grade student all decked out for the day," the Sister said.

Fr. Stanley bent over and hugged his old teacher. "It's been a while since we've seen each other. I've missed my favorite grade schoolteacher."

"Just look at you, Stan. All grown up and handsome as ever. Look at me. A dried-up old prune who has to get around by being pushed."

"You look like springtime to me. How have you been feeling, Sister Clarissa?"

"Oh, rotten as ever. I'm ready to leave this world behind. Getting old exposes all those joints you took for granted that have now come back screaming at you when you try to get around. That's how I'm paying for all of my old sins."

"Sins, my foot!" Stanley objected. You wouldn't know sin if it walked in and shook hands."

The Sister laughed. "Oh, Stanley! You always had such a sense of humor. Sit down on the chair and tell me how things have been going in Guatemala."

"Frankly, it's gotten rough. There's a war going on across the country. The government has sided with the large companies and the landowners against the people. Because the Church helps the poor, they are calling us Communists and subversives. Tragically, our Church is under attack."

"Yup! That's what I've been picking up. You know, Stan, that I keep up with you every day. I follow what you missionaries are doing out there in that wilderness. I know about the revolutionaries that are fighting the government."

"The country's president Fernando Romeo Lucas Garcia has turned on his own people. The military is attacking the Indians and religious. The situation is frightening."

"Just as I suspected. And there you are right in the middle of it all."

"Afraid so."

Sister Clarissa nodded. "Why'd you come back?"

"That's a good question. I'm not sure that I should have."

"In other words, those military people were after you too?"

"You never wasted much time in getting right to the point," Stanley said. "I guess you might say that some of the local folks thought I ought to take a little vacation."

"Vacation, indeed!" Sister Clarissa shook her head. "They wanted to get you out of the firing range because you are a prime target."

"You might say that." Stanley grinned. "Actually, that's one of the reasons that I wanted to talk with you. I have to consider what my next step should be. No one wants me to go back."

Sister Clarissa shook her head. "They're all apprehensive for you, aren't they?"

"Afraid so."

"I understand. I would be concerned too."

"That's why I need some of your sage advice. You kept me going when seminary had nearly finished me off. I need to hear what you think."

"Stan, I have often quoted the Cure of Ars to you. St. Jean Vianney lived in a similar time of revolution and upheaval in France just like what you are facing. He would have understood your dilemma like no one else. But St. Jean never turned back. He faced the challenge with resolute faith. I believe he would tell you to do the same. Remember! When Jesus called us to follow him, he called us to come and die."

"Would you do that?"

"If I could get out of this wheelchair, I'd be there in a minute."

Stanley laughed. "I believe you would."

"Father, you're the only one who knows what the Holy Spirit is calling you to do. Obedience is all that is required. I know you will be faithful to that call."

"Thank you, Sister Clarissa. That's what I needed to hear."

PART THREE

"If anyone would come after me, he must deny himself and take up his cross and follow me. For whoever wants to save his life will lose it, but whoever loses his life for me will find it.
--Matthew 16:24-25

34

"Archbishop Salatka has been looking forward to seeing you," the secretary said. "Please go on in."

Stanley turned the knob and walked in. The archbishop immediately jumped from his chair and came around the desk. "Father! So good to see you. Sit down."

Fr. Stanley sat down in a large, cushioned chair across from the bishop. "My boy, I hope your visit home has been good."

"Most positive. I have enjoyed seeing my family and Sister Marita so much. We were always close."

"Marvelous folks," the archbishop said. "I've always appreciated all of them." He sat down on the edge of his seat. "I must be honest with you, Fr. Stanley. I have checked with the State Department about conditions in Guatemala and they are warning American citizens not to go there. They believe the country is unsafe."

Fr. Stanley nodded his head. "I know," he said softly.

"You are aware of these unstable conditions."

"Yes, I am."

"And so, what are you thinking?"

Fr. Rother smiled. "Certainly, makes my decision more difficult but I know what my people are living with. Many are being severely harassed by the military. I'm afraid some have been killed. The government doesn't like the indigenous people."

"But you have an associate who can carry on the work."

"My current right- hand man is of Indian descent. Any others would probably be the same. They have the same vulnerability except that I am an American. I think the military fears Americans more. I am taller than any of them. Makes me an easier target."

The archbishop leaned back in his chair and folded his hands under his chin. He looked particularly thoughtful. "You know that they will kill you."

"Yes, I know."

The afternoon sunlight poured through the windows, casting shadows over the archbishop's office and sending a reflection from the large Crucifix hanging on the side wall. Shelves loaded with books seemed to fade away under the bright light. Outside the cold winds of winter continued to blast against the brick walls. A few flakes of snow bounced against the windows.

Fr. Stanley nodded. "You are correct. The Tz'utujil people that I serve are trapped between a defensive government that cares little for the citizens and rebels who are fighting to oust the current regime. Both sides have a great deal to lose."

"And we don't want to lose *you!*"

The conversation continued into the afternoon, but the archbishop could see that Fr. Stanley's mind was made up. He had already made a noble and brave decision and the archbishop knew he couldn't stand between this good man and his destiny. Of course,

Fr. Stanley had already avoided being captured and he might well do so again. His straightforward disposition carried its own cleverness. Surely, he would find his way through the jungle of assaults and attacks. That was what he had to depend on.

"So, I guess the matter is settled," the archbishop said.

"I've always been a farm boy at heart. I guess one of the ideas that stayed with me from the scripture is that the good shepherd doesn't run when danger threatens. I can't retreat because the situation might become perilous. The Tz'utujil people have become my flock. Regardless of the cost, I must stand with them."

The archbishop nodded slowly. Seldom had he seen such fidelity. There was nothing more he could say.

***

Stanley had lived in that upstairs room even before the time he was a teenager. The walls still had yellowed clippings from his days in FFA. The picture of him standing with the angus bull he raised remained thumb-tacked to the wall. Today, the blue ribbon he received at the county fair seemed even more nostalgic. For their own reasons, his parents had left the room just as it was the day he walked out. The truth was that all of these mementos were symbols of the past. Like objects in a museum, they were part of yesterday where he could no longer live. Their value today was reminders of what he stood for. The simplicity and goodness of the past helped to underscore the rightness of the decision he had made. It was time to go.

"What are you doing?" Sister Marita asked from the doorway.

"I'm packing my bag," Stanley said. "I'll be leaving soon."

She said nothing. Her thoughts were written in her face.

"Don't have much to take with me."

"Have you told Mom and Dad yet?"

"No. No, I'm waiting until this afternoon. I thought it would be easier for all of us to not drag things out."

"Yes, yes, that's true. Your leaving will be hard for all of us. I've invited Tom and his wife over for supper. That'll make everything easier."

Stanley smiled. "Betty Mae, you think of everything."

"Everything?" Tears welled up in her eyes. "I'm afraid so."

***

The smell of cooking beef wound through all the rooms in the house. Gertrude had always been a superb cook, but her pot roast and vegetables were always a favorite of the entire family. A huge bowl of mashed potatoes with a smaller ladle of gravy stood on the side at in the center of the table. The steaming heap of sauerkraut had come out of the cabbage in the garden last summer. There was always a container of corn left over from the Fall harvest. Family get togethers were always celebrated with a meal fit for a monarch.

When the knock came on the front door, Stanley immediately rushed forward.

"Tom!" Stanley swung the door open and reached out to hug his brother and Tom's wife Marti as well. "Super that you could come tonight!

"Never miss one of Mom's suppers," Tom said. "Good for my waist." The brothers laughed and kept shaking hands.

"You're still out there farming like an old son of the red dirt?" Stanley said.

"It's in my blood," Tom answered. Can't get away from sitting on a tractor."

"How well I know," Stanley agreed. "I still love the smell of an old engine running. Come on in and sit down."

The family gradually assembled around the table. Sister Marita kept bringing in glasses of iced tea. Franz stood there beaming at his assembled family. While he didn't say much, his pride remained obvious. Once everything was ready. Gertrude came in with her apron still on.

"I believe we are ready for the blessing," Gertrude said. "Stanley, please lead us."

For years, the family had prayed the same prayer. He smiled and the words just naturally tumbled from his mouth. "Bless us O Lord and these thy gifts which we are about to receive from thy bounty. Through Christ our Lord. Amen." Stanley looked up and smiled. "Dig in!"

The family laughed and began passing the bowls around. Everyone joked about eating too much and that Betty Mae ate too little. They talked of the winter wheat that looked promising for the Spring. Everyone agreed more rain would be needed that would probably start coming in April. Tom related having sold some livestock at a good price. Looked like the market for beef would remain high.

"And what about you, Stan?" Tom asked. "Thinking of taking a parish here in Oklahoma."

Stanley smiled and shook his head. "No, I don't think so."

"Well, where are you going next?" Tom asked.

"I'll be going back to Santiago Atitlan, to my regular parish." Stan said quietly.

"What?" Tom frowned and laid his fork down. "Going back?"

"Yes, the parish is expecting me to return."

"Son, there's great danger down there," Franz said.

"Dad, I guess there's danger everywhere. If I took a parish in say ... a place ... a ... like Chicago. There'd be the same problems everywhere. That's the times in which we live."

"I know," Tom said, "but we keep hearing that Guatemala is embroiled in a war."

"Well, there's trouble in the country. Sure, but I live out in the countryside, in the trees, in the jungle."

"Isn't that where the fighting is happening?" Tom's wife Marti asked.

Stanley nodded but didn't say anything.

"Holy Trinity Church prays for you every Sunday," Tom said. "The parish remains concerned about your well-being."

"Oh, I'm going to be fine, but tell the folks to keep praying. Never hurts," Stanley joked.

Betty Mae looked at him sternly. "No, it doesn't."

Franz and Gertrude glanced at each other but said nothing. For several moments, no one spoke. Quietness settled around the table.

Finally, Tom asked. "Well, Stan. When are you thinking of going back?"

He took a deep breath. "Tomorrow. Tomorrow afternoon."

Gertrude gasped. Franz mouth dropped slightly.

"My people have some immediate needs that I must take care of. I told everyone that I would be back in time for Holy Week. We don't have that many days left in Lent. We must get prepared for Palm Sunday. They are important days for us." He smiled at everyone. "So, I must leave tomorrow."

Tears filled Gertrude's eyes as well as Betty Mae's. Franz could only stare.

Tom finally said, "Glad you gave us plenty of warning." He grinned. "After all what's 24 hours give or take a little."

"Oh, I'll be back soon," Stanley said. "Just got to get our house in order down there."

Gertrude reached for her son's hand and squeezed it. "What can we say? We don't want you to go."

Stanley looked away. "I must."

35

The airplane circled above Guatemala City and then turned toward the La Aurora Airport in Finta San Isidro that served the area. The airport wasn't large, and the terminal had only a few gates. When they landed, an attendant pushed up a metal staircase for the passengers to walk down to the tarmac. Fr. Stanley walked inside dressed just as he left the country and carrying the same bag by his side. Passport control proved to be only functional, and few people were inside the terminal.

Stanley looked around. He had sent word to the rectory for Father Adan to pick him at Finta San Isidro. He could drive the red Ford pickup and they would quickly be on their way back to Santiago Atitlan. Stanley glanced around the building, but he didn't see Fr. Adan anywhere. He started walking slowly toward the front door.

"*Por favor,* "a man walked to Stanley. "I will drive you."

Fr. Stanley looked twice. This guy definitely was not Fr. Adan.

"Looking for someone?" Fr. Stanley mumbled in Spanish.

"*Si,* " the short man said. "Fr. Adan will not be here today. I am taking his place."

"What?"

"Bishop Angelico Melotto moved Fr. Adan because of the death threats on his life." He extended his hand. "I am your new associate. My name is Father Pedro Bocel. I am a Cakchiquel Indian."

"Well, my goodness! Glad to meet you Fr. Bocel." Stanley shook his hand warmly. "Frankly, I was looking for a different person."

"Of course. Most of us look alike. Short, dark-skinned people. You are nearly six-foot-tall and tower over all of us. No one could miss you. Fair-skinned and large. You stand out like the last stock of corn in the fall."

Stanley laughed. "That's true. I am taller than about anyone else. I guess the soldiers can spot me instantly."

"I'm sure they will report that you have returned. The pickup is outside. We can simply walk by them nonchalantly and drive away."

"Okay. All I've got is this one bag. Let's go."

The two priests walked slowly down the hall and out the front door where two soldiers stood just outside holding military rifles. Fr. Stanley nodded a friendly smile, but the soldiers only stared. The priests kept walking. Once they were in the truck, they pulled away with no problems. Soon they were out of town and back on the dirt road that led to Santiago Atitlan.

"If Bishop Melotto moved Fr. Adan, the situation must have gotten worse," Fr. Stanley said.

"I'm sorry to say that this is so. The insurgents have made gains, and this only further threatens the government. They believe the natives are opposed to them and that is true. Consequently, they kill indiscriminately. All across the country, our people are being attacked."

"What about our congregation of Saint James the Apostle?"

"People are worried. They knew it was wise of you to leave the country, but still they are frightened. When they discover that you have returned, there will be a great outpouring of love and joy that you have returned. Your coming back will give them new hope."

"Good. As soon as they know I'm back in town, we can start getting ready for a great Palm Sunday celebration."

"Oh, my! People will come from everywhere to join us," Fr. Bocel said. "I'm sure the entire city of Santiago Atitlan will rejoice."

They drove on silently. Stanley knew the military would take particular note of a large demonstration on Palm Sunday. Such an event could not be hidden.

***

Fr. Stanley walked into the rectory dining hall and set his bag down. For the first time, he realized how this wooden building felt like home. The familiar smell of the kitchen, the lingering scent of the exposed timbers all blended in a welcome home song. He laughed and remembered the times he had sat at one of the tables with the red and white checkered table clothes and talked with some of the Sisters. The large room had that "farm table" feeling that always made him feel at home.

"Padre Francisco!" The brothers Diego and Nicolas Chavez burst into the rectory. "We heard you had come back. Welcome home."

"Thank you," Fr. Stanley said. "Good to see you."

"We wanted you to know that we finished the work on the retablo," Diego Chavez said. "We put in the additions that you described. We think you will like it."

"Oh, I know I will. We will want to recognize your work before the entire congregation on Sunday and thank you in public."

"Thank you." Diego said. Both men bowed several times.

"I know you will want to be paid."

"Only when it is convenient," Nicolas said.

"I just got here. So, I'll have to pay you in the morning."

"Certainly," Diego said. "We will be here early."

"I bet you will," Stanley chuckled.

The two brothers left, and he picked up his bag to take it upstairs. His new associate came in the dining hall. "This communique came in while you were gone," Fr. Bocel said. "Apparently, you met with the Sisters from the Carmelite Missionaries of St. Teresa before I came and they made an offer to you. Here's their response." He handed Fr. Stanley the sheet of paper.

"Oh!" He read it slowly. "Ah, they have accepted my counterproposal to do some work with them. Excellent."

"Do you feel like you are home?" Fr. Bocel asked.

"Yes. Yes. I do."

36

The old red pickup pulled up in front of the rectory. Fr. Stanley got out and lifted a large sack of flour out of the back. He began carrying the heavy sack into the rectory. Several children gathered and followed him. Stanley set the flour down on the steps and sat down. The little boys rushed forward and started pulling on his long legs.

"Hey! What are you doing to me?"

The children laughed. "Come play soccer with us."

"I think I'm a little old for you guys," Stanley said.

"Oh, no," one of the children protested. "We will outrun you." He threw the worn ball at Stanley.

Stanley grabbed it. "Okay, here we go." He started back down the steps.

"Padre Francisco!" Father Pedro Bocel called from the doorway. "Need to talk with you immediately."

"Sorry, guys." He tossed the ball back to the little boys. "Got to talk with my buddy. See you later."

He hurried back up the steps and walked inside. "What's going on?"

Fr. Bocel motioned for him to sit down at one of the dining tables. "I just got a message from Bishop Melotto. He is warning us that the government is silently approving and promoting death squads. They call themselves *Mano Blanco*, the white hand. The Bishop wants us to know how dangerous these men are and to be on the lookout for them."

"I see," Fr. Stanley said slowly. "A new threat."

"The government is using every possible means to attack. We must be vigilant."

"Thank you, Fr. Bocel. We must inform everyone about this problem."

"I have already sent some messengers into Santiago Atitlan to spread the word."

"Good. Excellent. Let's watch and see what follows."

***

During the following three days, conflicting messages kept coming in. Empty threats were spread among the natives. No one knew what to believe. The news that Padre Francisco, who they often called Padre Aplas, had returned was about the only positive report heard throughout the area. Stanley listened to the reports and tried to discern the truth, but it was not easy. Every day someone rushed in with the latest dire story that turned out not to be true.

Fr. Bocel rushed in from the town. "I know what's coming for sure. I picked this up from some fruit merchants who usually know the inside story. They have heard that a group called ORPA, which means Organization of the People at Arms, are preparing to come marching into Santiago Atitlan. This cadre says they are going to gather in front of our church and make speeches They are organizing everybody to attend. Looks like this is for real."

"Okay. I guess we better get ready for a demonstration. Let's go outside and see."

"A crowd is already forming. We can blend in with the people. I am ready to go if you are."

The two men went out of the rear door of the rectory and walked along the back path. When they turned the corner, they could see people standing around talking and waiting to see what would happen. Off in the distance the beat of a drum echoed through the town. The constant boom, boom, boom grew louder. People began running here and there. Mothers holding their small babies emerged from the doorways. Farmers in their white cowboy hats started walking in. In a few minutes, the crowd tripled in size.

Down the main street of Santiago Atitlan, men dressed in regular clothes began marching in carrying rifles and large machete knives. Their formation signaled they were an organized militia, and everyone knew the ORPA had come to town. These make-shift soldiers marched into the plaza in front of St. James the Apostle Church and filled the square. One of the soldiers in the front walked up the church steps.

"*Amigos!*" the man shouted. "We have come to tell you that liberation and hope is on the way. All across our great country, citizens are gathering to fight the oppressive government we have suffered under. The time for revolt is at hand. Let us stand together."

The militia soldiers began cheering. Some of the people joined in. Others stood silently.

He continued, "The government of President Ferdinando Romeo Luis Garcia had been oppressing you for years. He has stolen from the farmers and cheated you in the marketplace. You know about his crimes. He does not like the native people and makes deals with foreign governments that are only to his advantage. There is no end to his crimes. He must be taken down."

Once more the soldiers cheered. A large number of the townspeople clapped.

"We have come to tell you that his evil deeds will soon end. When the great people of Guatemala refuse to accept his lies and confront him, then the end will be close at hand. Are you ready to join us in this final battle?

As on cue, the militia began firing their rifles in the air. The roar frightened the small children and the babies. Crying broke out among the crowd, but the militia kept shooting in the air.

"You can join us with acts of resistance and sabotage," the leader shouted. "Shoot the government troops when they march into your city! Stop serving this corrupt government and help bring down President Garcia! There are more of us than there are of them!"

Once more the big bass drum roared out the booming beat. The soldiers saluted the people and turned, marching out the way they had come. The parade remained peaceful and most of the citizens remained silent watching the men leave their town. Fr. Stanley and Fr. Bocel stood silently watching the crowd disperse. When most of the people had returned to their homes, Fr. Stanley spoke in a quiet voice.

"It's easy to march in here and call for war, but our people don't have weapons and fighting is the last thing they are interested in. They are farmers and only want to work the fields. That sort of rabble-rousing will only get our people killed."

Fr. Bocel nodded his agreement. "This demonstration was peaceful today, but the results could be very dangerous. We have not seen the last of this situation."

"Indeed! You can bet the government will know by tomorrow morning that the ORPA was here. All this will do is call attention to our town and the Solol`a region. That's very dangerous."

The two priests turned back toward the rectory walking silently. Natives nodded and smiled as they walked by, but most people headed for home. Behind them the *Fuego* volcano sent a column of smoke curling up into the sky. Stanley watched the smoke float across the mountains.

He said softly. "Let's hope no one gets burned."

37

Only a few weeks after the ORPA march through Santiago Atitlan, a letter came from the Bishop of Solola Guatemala, Angelico Melotto. Fr. Stanley assembled the mission staff to hear the message. The Sisters and Fr. Bocel sat around the dining tables covered with red and white table clothes. Fr. Stanley stood to one side after explaining why thy had gathered. He could see everyone was nervous.

Fr. Pedro Bocel held up the letter. "Our local bishop wants us to know what is happening across the country. He remains deeply concerned for our wellbeing. Here is what Bishop Meletto has written to each of us."

The acts of violence among us have taken on unimaginable forms: for there are murders, kidnappings, torture, and even desecrations of the victim's bodies. We pastoral agents are constantly watched. Our sermons are taped, and our every activity is checked. In a country basically Catholic, three priests have recently been murdered and another kidnapped. Several other priests and religious are threatened with death and others have been expelled from the country. For us there is special significance in the circumstances surrounding the violent death of Father Jose Maria Gran Ciera, shot in the back while returning home on horseback.

A part of this religious persecution is the campaign of discredit and slander aimed at certain bishops, priests, and religious, a campaign that tends to create a climate of distrust in the body of the faithful toward the legitimate pastors. The very priests who have offered their lives as martyrs for Christ, in preaching the Gospel, have been afterward the objects of insidious calumnies meant to blacken their obvious Christian witness.

Fr. Bocel choked, stopped, and laid the letter down. Fr. Stanley walked back to the center of the room.

"My friends, this is what we are up against. I am certain that the demonstration in front of our church has been called to the attention of the government. Even though we have been in the background and have no involvement whatsoever in this revolt, the military will now be looking at us with a jaundiced eye. We must recognize that we are in the midst of an ongoing war and the Church has become a major target. The situation will get worse before it gets better. I wanted you to know the circumstances we are facing in the on-going days. The times will be treacherous. If any of you want to leave, please feel that you have the freedom to do so without any pressure to stay or receive ill-will from any of us. The time to leave is now."

One of the native Sisters held up her hand. "We have surrendered our lives to Jesus Christ. He is our life. The government does not understand this fact. They cannot frighten us to retreat. We are here for the long haul." She sat down.

"Does anyone have anything more to say?" Fr. Stanley looked around the room. No one moved and he smiled. "Well, I guess we are all in this struggle together. Thank you for your tenacity. We will need to maintain constant surveillance and keep our door locked. Let's not go out alone. We will need to keep a sharp eye out for any strangers and observe what the military seems to be about. We must spend as much time as possible participating in the Mass and praying constantly for each other. Let it be said and be known that our motto is "To God be the glory."

Someone clapped and then the whole room broke out in applause.

***

Fr. Stanley was preparing for an afternoon Catechism class when Fr. Pedro broke in. "Did you hear the engines?"

For a moment, Fr. Stanley listened. "No, but I do now. What's going on?"

The Guatemalan military is roaring into our town on motorcycles. The are all over the place and seem to be coming to the plaza in front of our church. You can watch but should keep a distance from them."

"Okay," Stanley said. "Why don't you dress like a native and walk around listening to what they are doing."

Fr. Pedro nodded his head. "I will. We need to go right now."

The two priests took the rear door again to appear less obvious. Fr. Stanley found an obscure niche between two of the buildings and slipped into the space. Fr. Bocel threw a sa*rape* over his shoulders and walked into the small crowd. The soldiers were corralling the town's people and pushing them into the large plaza.

Soldiers kept herding people around and screaming at them. The people looked frightened.

"Were you at this illegal demonstration?" One of the military men barked in the face of a local man.

The native said nothing but kept shaking his head.

"Speak up!" the soldier demanded.

"N-no. No."

"Don't lie to me!" the officer growled.

"No sir, No sir."

The officer whirled around and confronted the woman standing next to them. "Were you here?"

She shook her head.

"Yes, I can see that none of you were around. The rebels must have been here all alone talking to themselves." He leaned into the women's face. "Who works at the radio station?"

She shrugged.

"Don't act innocent with me." I said, "Who works at the radio station.?"

"Some people I don't know," she said.

The man pushed her back. "I bet you don't know anything, you stupid women."

Pedro Bocel slipped away and walked back through the large crowd that had now assembled. Another military official and had pushed one of the local men up against the adobe covered building.

"Who applauded?" he yelled in the man's face. "Who clapped when the leader spoke?"

"I-I d-don't know. I-I was working in the field."

"You are a liar," the soldier charged. "Now speak up."

"I-I don't know nobody."

The officer swung his fist into the farmer's face and slung him to the ground. "You are lucky I didn't kill you today." The soldier walked on to the next person.

"What about the people with the church?" the man asked one of the little women. "Were they in the gathering?"

"I don't know. I didn't see any of them." She cowered and tried to stand back.

"Were the priests out here promoting the rally?" The soldier stared into her face.

"I told you that I didn't see any of them." She held up her hand in case he struck her face.

Fr. Bocel kept moving cautiously through the crowd. The military clearly wanted the names of anyone who had supported the rally.

One soldier had pinned Diego Chavez against a black car. "I want the truth," the soldier kept hollering. "Were people from the church involved in the demonstration?"

"No." Diego kept shaking his head.

"The priest? We're they down there with the ORPA crowd?"

Diego shook his head again. The soldier slapped him across the face so hard that his nose began to bleed.

"I don't think you are hearing my question." He hit him again.

Diego doubled and fell to his knees. The officer swung his knee into the native's face, sending him sprawling on the plaza. Pedro Bocel backed away and slipped behind three men standing nearby. The interrogation continued for thirty more minutes before the military got back on their motorcycles and drove away. The crowd began to disperse, and Fr. Stanley and his associate returned to the rectory.

"What do you make of what we just saw?" Pedro asked.

"This town's now on their radar," Stanley said. "I think they particularly wanted two things: who supported the rally and were any of us behind it. Obviously, they wanted to implicate the Church."

Pedro shook his head. "Hard times are ahead. Very hard."

38

Have any of the soldiers come back?" Fr. Stanley asked his associate.

"No," Fr. Bocel said. "So far our streets are clear, but the people are worried."

"They should be. This guerilla war is far from ended. I know the military will be back. It's just a question of when they will show up."

Fr. Bocel shrugged. "Afraid so. You are working on the materials for the Sacraments of Initiation and first Holy Communion?"

"Yes. While we still have time left, we must bring in as many candidates as possible. I am anticipating we will have hundreds of responses. The people know they must seek the help of Almighty God in times like the one we are now in. Of course, we will receive them during the Feast of St. James."

"That's only two weeks away," Fr. Bocel said. "I know we'll have a great time.

The Fiesta turned out to be a great celebration. Children played clapped, and enjoyed the music from the mariachis with violins and guitars providing old Spanish songs along with their own native sounds. Mid-day a parade marched through the town with men carrying the statues of saints, now dressed in special vestments. The event played on into the night. At least for the day, the threats and worries vanished.

Once more with summer approaching, volunteers came from America. Earlier Stanley had developed a friendship with Father Joseph Moore who served in Oklahoma. The priest had a special heart for the work of the Guatemalan mission. Sensing that he could help, the priest came down.

"You are a brave man, Father Joseph" Fr. Stanley said. "Things have been a little tense around here."

"That's what I like," The priest joked. "Nothing like a little excitement to keep us busy."

"More than a little frivolity. You need to make sure you are protecting yourself around here."

"Sure thing," Joseph said. "Now, tell me what I can do to help you."

"How about celebrating a few Masses for us?"

"Excellent! Right up my alley."

In the evening, the two men talked about the Church and their perspective viewpoints. They discussed the changes that continued to unfold from Vatican II. Stanley discussed the threat that the government had been making against the church and how the natives were responding. The hospital continued taking care of the sick, and the radio broadcast religious messages, but avoided the news or any report that could bring retribution. Fr. Stanley found the exchanges with an American priest to be stimulating and updating. The days seemed to fly by.

"You are leaving today," Stanley said factually but his words sounded heavy and reluctant."

"Afraid so," Joseph said. "You know I use my vacation days to come down here. I find it more refreshing than any vacation to a random place. I love this mission."

"And we love having you."

"I'll be back," he said. "Ya'll hear," his Oklahoma accent popped out.

They waved as the pickup drove off to the airport.

Fr. Stanley walked back into the rectory and sat down at one of the long dining tables. He poured himself a cup of coffee and thought about his friend's visit. Their time sharing their thoughts and reflections had meant a great deal to him. He would miss this old friend.

"Padre Francisco!" Jose Mendez, an indigenous parishioner, broke in through the front door. "I must speak with you."

"Jose, come over here and sit down. What's up?"

"There are strangers coming into the town. We have seen people on the street that no one knows. We are concerned."

"Strangers? That's not good?"

"Oh, no," Jose said. "Everybody knows everybody, but there are strange faces."

"What do they seem to want?"

"They ask questions of the people. Some of these men even stop people on the street and press them for answers. They want to know about the church, the radio station. They try to find out who the leaders of the people are. They ask questions about you, Padre."

"Just as I feared."

"These spies want to know about people joining the church. They ask for names. It is not a good sign."

"Let's go out and take a look. Meet some of these strangers."

"I don't know," Jose sounded hesitant. "I am very uneasy about these intrusions."

"Let's see what they say to me." Fr. Stanley stood up. "You don't have to go with me."

"I think I'd rather not. I'm not afraid." His eyes looked down and he clinched his jaw. "I think I'd better stay here."

"Okay," Fr. Stanley said. "I'll just take a leisurely stroll through Santiago Atitlan and see what I find."

Wearing his native hand-woven vest and a plain blue shirt, he started walking past the plaza in front of the church and down one of the narrow town streets. He didn't have to go two blocks before he recognized one of the strangers talking with a local man.

"Padre," the villager called out. "This man is asking me questions."

The stranger turned and eyed the priest. Short like the villagers, Stanley towered above him. He started backing away.

"You have some questions for us?" Fr. Stanley called out.

The man turned and virtually ran back into the town.

"What do you think? Fr. Stanley asked the native.

"These men mean real trouble," the man said.

"They obviously don't like me," the priest said. "We must keep an eye on them."

"People are going to leave. I know because they tell me. The whole town is alarmed. They will try to cross the lake and reach Panajachel at night. Many will take the bus to Guatemala City and try to disappear. Some are considering hiding in the mountains. Our friends know these men are a bad sign of what is to come."

Fr. Stanley shook his head. "I understand but we can't leave because we are frightened. We must stand firm."

The man blinked several times. "Thank you." He turned and hurried away.

The priest knew what he was thinking. Many would do the same. They were scared.

39

The sun slipped up over the mountains spreading a blazing red over the trees and the thick foliage around Santiago Atitlan. The people had already begun to move around the streets. Burros plotted along with bundles of sticks or large clay jugs hanging from their backs. Usually, the early morning streets were a simple, quiet beginning of another day as the citizens went about their chores. Today a different atmosphere hung in the narrow walkways between the houses and buildings. The natives hurried rather than walking slowly. Citizens seemed agitated and uneasy. Tension hung in the atmosphere.

Fr. Stanley sat in the rectory reviewing the plans and the layout of the church property. He carefully studied all the entry and exist points. There were doors that needed to be secured and gates made secure. The casual come-and-go atmosphere was over. Now everything had to be checked and rechecked.

Fr. Pedro Bocel knocked and then walked in. "Been checking the outside doors. I think the locks are adequate."

"Good. I've been looking at the plans of the grounds and the rectory. I think it would be better for me to move my bedroom. Sleeping upstairs has been fine, but I am next to a wooden wall.

From what I've learned, a hand grenade would shatter wood. I need a rock wall behind me."

"Absolutely," Fr. Bocel agreed. "The downstairs wall will be much better."

"I'm going to use a downstairs room that I'll turn into my living room. I'll put in a pull-out sofa that will make into a bed. I believe that will also make life a little safer for the Sisters. They can move also from the convent if they wish."

Pedro Bocel nodded. "Agreed. Now I must tell you what happened two days ago. I had been broadcasting from our radio station when I left to come back to the rectory. As I strolled down the street, I sensed something was wrong and glanced over my shoulder. A man was following me."

"You're certain?"

"Yes, whoever this was kept the same distance from behind me. When I reached the rectory, he disappeared. Then, this morning I was back at the radio station. When I looked out the window, I saw three men in a dark car waiting at the edge of the station. I knew they were waiting for me to come out. I prayed and threw a *serape* over my shoulders. I had to walk in front of the car to leave. The men in the car didn't recognize me. Father, I tell you that it was a miracle that nothing happened."

"Indeed!"

"Then those men realized they had made a big mistake. The car started up and they came after me. I rushed into a store to hide. The car went past and then turned around and came back very slowly. My friend who owned the store watched them go back and forth until they disappeared. I guess they finally drove off. I can't decide whether they were trying to frighten me or meant to attack."

Fr. Stanley wiped his mouth nervously. "At the very least, that wasn't a good sign. The military is definitely keeping an eye on us. I wonder if any of this would have happened if you had not been walking alone."

"Your guess is as good as mine."

"I know my Archbishop in Oklahoma City is aware of these conditions, but I must keep him updated. Right now, I am going to write him and make sure that he known fully what's going on."

"Good idea," Fr. Bocel said. "Please let me know how he responds."

"Sure."

Fr. Stanley pulled out a portable typewriter he kept near his desk and began to write."

Dear Archbishop,

As you know, there have been four priests killed in this country. All have been foreign, but none have been from the United States. The Diocese of Quiche, to the North of Solola, has been abandoned completely. The bishop even left the diocese. Two priests were killed, catechists, lay people, etc., were killed and the rest of the priests left to stay alive. The repression continues and at one place there were at least 60 men of the church lined up by the wall and they killed every fourth person.

The country is in rebellion, and they are taking it out on the church. Some say the Diocese of Solola where the mission is located is the next on their list for persecution. They are not letting up.

    Your faithful servant,

        Fr. Stanley Rother.

Stan reread the letter and then sealed the envelope. He had to get it on its way.

***

That evening Fr. Bocel returned from the town. The two priests ate supper together.

"I can tell you that the military is everywhere now. A few of the soldiers wear camouflaged suits some of the time, but you can see them standing on the street corners. Many of the military are carrying submachine guns. They don't say anything, but they are scaring the people to death."

"I know," Fr. Stanley said. "I'm not sure whether they are trying to intimidate everyone or might be preparing for an attack. Of course, the people don't have weapons that are even near what the military is carrying. We are at their mercy."

Fr. Bocel glanced around the room to make sure no one was listening. "I must admit that I have become fearful. I think they are after us. You and me!"

Stanley nodded his head. "Yes, I believe that is true. Listen, my friend. You have been a good associate and I know you care about the people. At the same time, I don't want you to feel any pressure to stay here. You can return to where you came from with my blessing."

"Why do you stay, Fr. Stanley? You could go back to America and leave all of this troubled world behind."

"There is a passage that keeps running through my mind from the Gospel of St. John. 'I am the good shepherd. The good shepherd lays down his life for his sheep... I know my sheep and they know me.' Pedro, I must stay because I am a shepherd for the Tz'utujil people. I cannot leave them."

"Thank you. I needed to hear those words."

Stanley reached out and put his hand on the man's shoulder. "Let me pray for you. Dear heavenly Father, please help both of us to walk the path you have given us. As you show us the way, give us the strength to be faithful to your call. We have no hope but you. In the name of the Father, the Son, and the Holy Spirit. Amen."

Tears fill Pedro Bocel's eyes. "Thank you. I needed that prayer."

40

Fr. Pedro Bocel stuck his head out of the rectory door. "Padre Francisco! You have an important telephone call from Guatemala City!"

"Okay," Stanley turned from the child he had been playing ball with. "I'm coming in." These days he knew that careful attention had to be paid to any outside contact. He walked into the rectory. "Who is this?" he asked abruptly.

"Well, well, you did come back." The familiar voice of Fr. Ron Curtain echoed through the telephone line. "I thought I told you not to."

"Is this that nervous pest, Fr. Ron Curtain?"

"Ah, you always have that sense of humor."

"What's going on?"

"You will understand if I am brief and not explicit. You need to be in Guatemala City tomorrow. *El Presidente* is going to make a speech. You should be in the crowd and listen. Don't come looking like a priest. Just dress like a good old boy." After a long pause, Fr. Curtain added, "It's going to be *very* important for all of us to be there. Don't say anything back to me. Just show up." The phone went silent.

Stanley stared at the dead telephone and then slowly hung up. "Guess I better go."

***

Because of his height, Fr. Stanley tried to step next to one of the trees in the plaza that shielded him from view to some extent. The crowd had already begun to form. Military police were everywhere. Stanley pressed his back against a large tree and tried to slink down.

"What's an American doing in this crowd?"

Stanley jumped. "What?" Fr. Ron Curtain laughed. "It's good that you came. My sources tell me that good old President Ferdinando Garcia is going to up the ante. Keep your ears open." Fr. Curtain walked away.

Off in the distance drums began to roll out a steady beat. A band struck up a stirring march. People started to clap. Men in general's uniforms began to assemble on the balcony in the government palace in front of them. Attaches started filling up the platform. The band marched in under the balcony and stopped playing. When *Presidente* Garcia came out, an uproar of applause exploded. Decked out in the finest uniform with medals across his chest and a blue sash running down the front, the dictator looked supreme. Citizens cheered and applauded.

"Get ready," Ron slipped back alongside the tree and whispered. "The show is about to start."

"Amigos! Ciudadanos!" Ferdinando Garcia waved to the crowd. "Thank you for your support!"

The crowd continued to cheer. Fr. Stanley glanced around. On all sides the soldiers stood with pointed guns. *They aren't kidding*, Stanley thought.

The President held a sheet of paper in front of him and began reading. What he had to say sounded like the typical political propaganda that came out regularly in the newspapers. Then he stopped. For a moment, Ferdinando Garcia looked at the crowd with a silent stare. With a dramatic flourish, he flung the script over his shoulder. Fr. Stanley immediately sensed an artificial ploy.

"Amigos," Garcia leaned forward. "Let me speak from my heart. We are surrounded by enemies of the government. Vicious thugs who want to hurt our people and destroy the country. We have been forced to endure drastic measures to protect citizens. Yes, teachers and government officials have been forced to endure harsh measures so that order can be ensured. Obviously, this policy has been difficult for some, but others are protected. Now, I come to the most difficult part. We know that religious people are negatively catechizing the people and turning them against the government. They are responsible for the unrest in the countryside. They continue to create chaos. Now, I am a religious man myself, but I know heretics and apostates when I see them. I am reluctant to take action, but I need your support. I ask you my people, should we expel from our country these religious who are perverting the people?"

The crowd burst into spontaneous applause. Soldiers pushed their weapons aside and cheered wildly shouting their support. Stanley peeked around the side of the large tree and watched supporters waving their arms to drum up support. No question that this so-called "voluntary" response had been a well-planned demonstration from the beginning. There was no question in his mind that the call for expelling the religious included him.

"Gracias!" The President kept waving at the crowd. *"Gracias a ustedes!"* He kept waving until he turned and disappeared inside. The crowd began to disperse. Stanley looked around to see if he could find Fr. Curtain.

"What'd you think?" a voice said behind him.

Fr. Stanley jumped. "You came out of nowhere, Ron. A little unnerving."

"Did you hear the threat? Can you see where this is going? Now Ferando Garcia can claim he is only doing the will of the people when he loads you in a bus and dumps you out at the border. That's the easiest approach. The more likely strategy is that they start shooting all internationals."

Fr. Stanley took a deep breath. "They are already patrolling our streets in Santiago Atitlan. Soldiers are everywhere holding their submachine guns. People are scared to death. Many leave in the night."

"You've got an accurate picture. I cannot tell you how I know these things but trust me. The worst is ahead. I keep telling you to leave the country."

"I can't, Ron. I am the shepherd of this flock. If I leave to save my neck, it sends the signal that we are dependable only when it's safe. The people must know that the Church stands with them regardless of the circumstances. Our village church sat empty for a hundred years because the government ran all foreign nationals out. I can't let that happen again."

Fr. Curtain shook his head. "I knew that's what you would say. I just wanted to make sure you were adequately warned."

"Oh, I have the picture. Sure. I know what's probably ahead."

The American priest smiled. "I admire your bravery more than I can say."

"Oh, I am not some brave resistor. I'm just trying to be faithful to my vows. Why, back there in the beginning, I told Jesus Christ I'd stick around until he had other plans for me. He hasn't called me to any other place."

"We don't want to lose you." Tears welled up in the corners of Fr. Curtain's eyes. "Oh, dear God. Please keep your hand on my brother."

***

Stanley's old red truck chugged down the dusty road. He kept thinking over and over about what he had heard. But what did it really mean? Was Garcia only bluffing? Behind the fierce talk was he really losing ground? No one could tell him whether the rebels were making gains or not. They must be for the government to keep becoming more and more aggressive. Could the revolutionaries be closing in? Maybe that is what the President feared. No way to know and he didn't want to push Fr. Curtain any further. The priest undoubtedly knew far more than he was saying. Maybe not. He just couldn't be sure what the truth was. The simple fact was that no one knew for sure about anything. The indecision left him more worried than anything else.

41

All the way back to Santiago Atitlan, Fr. Stanley kept thinking about what he had heard in Guatemala City. He knew that danger was inevitable when he came back to the country but was it possible that the politicians were reacting to pressure more than relating facts. Did he hear only propaganda or was an assault imminent? As he pulled into the town, he thought probably both were true. The problem was that no one could tell him what to expect next.

And then there was his associate Fr. Pedro Bocel. Because his origins were Mayan, the military would certainly make him a target. Something had to be done and Stanley knew the circumstances demanded an immediate decision. He drove into the plaza in front of the rectory and stopped. He had to talk with Fr. Bocel tomorrow.

The sun had already begun to set and quiet prevailed across the church property. No one seemed to be lurking in the shadows at the moment. The seasons would soon change, and Easter would come again with a great celebration. He could only hope to be part of it. Fr. Stanley walked inside. He had an early morning Mass and needed to get to bed early. He shut the front door and locked it behind him.

***

A large number of the people had come to the first Mass of the day. Looking out over of the congregation, Fr. Stanley saw countless faces that he knew and cared about. These were good people. Simple in the ways of their fathers, and yet wise about so many more everyday practical matters. Their faces registered the tension that had fallen over the entire country. The liturgy continued to unfold.

Fr. Stanley walked to the pulpit. He began proclaiming the Gospel of John. "No one has greater love than the one who lays down his life for his friends. You are my friends if you do what I tell you."

The words rang in Stanley's ears. Something deep and profound rumbled within. He had read this passage many times, but this morning a different profundity rose up from within him that seemed almost impossible to grasp. With the realization came an abiding peace that transcended the worries that had settled like a dark cloud over the entire town. A knowing filled his mind with realizations that he could never express.

Fr. Stanley finished and said, "The Gospel of the Lord." The congregation responded, "Praise to you, Lord Jesus Christ."

Stanley stumbled through his brief sermon. He could see the words that he had written on a piece of paper, but his mind still remained absorbed with the scripture lesson. Somehow, he struggled through the homily and sat down. The Mass continued, and finally, it came time for him to walk to the altar. Words tumbled out of his mouth as if with a life of their own. "It is a good and joyful thing always and everywhere to give thanks to you Father Almighty, Creator of heaven and earth."

His words could not capture and express what surged from within his very being. Deep, deep within, his soul he reached out for a continuing encounter like a thirsty man grasping for a cup of cold water. Almost as if he were dreaming, Stanley sensed an even more profound meaning in the liturgy of the Holy Sacrifice. Here in this commemoration is where Jesus laid down his life. This is his blood and flesh being given up in the ultimate expression of perfect love. And now the Christ was again present at this altar, sacrificing for his friends. The realization, the memory, the moment, the encounter swept over Stanley like a great wave of compassion.

He lifted up the golden chalice. A sunbeam from one of the windows struck the rim with a sparkle of brilliant light. For a moment, Fr. Stanley's hands trembled as he slowly lowered the chalice to the altar. He had said the words of institution a thousand times, but today they had leaped off the page with a life of their own. Stanley knew he had crossed the bridge between the physical world and the transcendent realm of the divine. The Holy Spirit had captured his soul. A joy trembled within him that was also filled with pathos. He could barely hand the chalice and the paten to Fr. Bocel for him to administer the sacrament to the people that were moving forward to receive the elements. Stanley had to sit down to reconstitute himself. Never had he experienced such an overwhelming moment.

As the Mass concluded, Fr. Stanley knew he couldn't endure speaking with anyone. He had to stumble back to the sacristy and be alone. In those few moments at the altar, he felt as if he had been overwhelmed by the very reality of God. The encounter had to be fully absorbed and allowed to settle for him to be with people again. He dropped into a chair, took a deep breath, and closed his eyes.

***

That afternoon, Fr. Stanley called Pedro Bocel into the rectory office. The priest hurried in and sat down. "That was a moving Mass this morning," he said. "I noticed that you almost seemed to be someplace else."

Fr. Stanley smiled. "Lots of things are going on, my friend. We must talk about your situation."

Fr. Bocel shrugged. "I am happy here. No problems."

"I fear our days may be numbered. Because you are a full-blooded Cakchiquel Indian, you are considered an enemy of the government. If they attack us, you would be in their gunsights. I believe you must leave and return to a safer place. My friend, your life will be in danger if you remain here."

Pedro Bocel stiffened. "I have never asked to leave."

"Indeed!

You have been a man of honor who has worked here with distinction. Because I am responsible for you, I must act on your behalf. Moreover, we have become good friends. I will always treasure your friendship. I couldn't honor that relationship if I didn't have you leave for safety's sake."

Fr. Bocel stared at the floor. "I will always remember you as my dearest friend. I understand what you are saying, and I honor your words, but it is only with the deepest regret that I leave. But what about you? You are no safer than I am."

"I have no alternative but to be faithful to my flock. I have to stay."

"God help you." Fr. Bocel stood. "God bless you. I will be gone by tomorrow morning, but I will remember you always." He lunged forward and hugged his superior. "Thank you for all you have done for me." Fr. Bocel hurried out of the room as if he didn't want to express more emotion. The door closed silently behind him.

For a long time, Fr. Stanley sat quietly, saying nothing. He thought about how Pedro Bocel had been such a faithful, good man. There would always be a place for such a man. Other thoughts returned. The morning Mass had touched him deeply. Stanley felt like the Holy Spirit had imparted a new gift, a new understanding, a deeper perspective ... really more than he could describe or put into words. He had seen more than his eyes could behold. What would come next?

42

The sound began as a low rumble from somewhere far off like a movement of some order had begun. Those noises seeped through the rectory windows like the warning of an approaching storm. The usual quiet of the morning disappeared. Two of the Sisters rushed outside but saw nothing. Still, the roar grew louder. Stanley rolled over in bed and listened. For a few moments, he strained to make sense out of the racket; then the roar became familiar. He had heard tires and trucks going down the back road for years in Oklahoma. A caravan of military equipment was being sent to their town. He leaped out of bed. A big problem was coming down.

"What is happening?" one of the sisters asked when he rushed into the dining hall.

"Heavy equipment is being moved into Santiago Atitlan," Fr. Stanley answered. "I'm not sure what will come next but for the moment a convoy of this size means trouble. Make sure all the doors are locked. Tell everyone to stay inside until we get clarification. The sound is so loud because many trucks are being hauled in. Change of some sort is on the way."

"I will tell everyone," the Sister said. "Right now!"

The sound of engines increased. Motorcycles were coming toward the church property. The military appeared to be descending on the church compound.

One of the volunteer doctors ran out of the rectory. "Looks like they are coming to the hospital."

"I am not sure if they are attacking or terrorizing," Fr. Stanley said. "Appears they are about to surround the hospital. You better get over there. Because you are an American volunteer, I don't think they will give you any trouble. That may not be the case for the natives who work with us. Just keep telling the soldiers that you are an Americano"

The doctor started running toward the hospital.

Looks like we are under attack," Fr. Stanley thought. *"The military will be vicious."*

***

Gaspar Culan Yataz had once been a seminarian from the parish before he married. He became the director of the radio station *Voice of Atitlan* and was highly respected throughout the community. His program "Christ Calls You" aired three times a day and had significantly impacted the community. In the native community, Gaspar was recognized as a highly respected catechist. He and his wife Concepcion eventually settled in Panaj Canton. Now with their one-year-old baby, they were still in bed when a noise erupted outside.

Concepcion sat up in bed. She stared into the darkness. "What's that?"

"Huh?" Gaspar groaned and turned over.

The door flew open, and men rushed in.

"What?" Gaspar slung the covers aside, trying to see the shapes in the blackness.

Before he could stand, two men grabbed him and slung him to the door. Gaspar pushed back and tried to stand. "Help!" he screamed. "Somebody help us!"

The butt of a gun smashed into his chest. Gaspar tumbled to the floor, gasping for air. The man kicked him in the back.

"Finish him!" one of the intruders yelled. The two men began stomping Gaspar as hard as they could.

Gaspar doubled and could barely speak. "Go ahead," he sputtered. "Kill me quickly."

Concepcion grasped the baby Maria Linda and clutched her tightly. She rolled toward the hall trying to protect the child. She put her hand over Maria Linda's mouth to keep her from crying out loud but the baby still made a sound. A flashlight abruptly shot on and blared into her face. The blast of a pistol missed her only by inches and she fell backward against the wall.

"Get him out of here!" the leader yelled. "Put that noose around his neck!"

Concepcion peeked in horror above the edge of the bed. She could see Gaspar being dragged out of the door by the rope while one of the men pulled him by the arm.

"Get him out here! the demand echoed through the door.

Concepcion huddled in the darkness. Finally, the sound of men running died out. Slowly she laid the baby on the bed and crept toward the door. When she looked out, Concepcion could see nothing except the trail in the dirt where Gaspar's body had been dragged away. She flipped on the light switch. Splattered blood stains ran down the wall with a trail of blood stretching toward the open door. The silence became ominous.

Trembling and shaking, Concepcion slowly shrank into the chair next to the only table in the house. she wailed, "I will never see Gaspar again".

***

The sun had already risen when Concepcion and tiny Maria Linda arrived at the mission. She beat on the front door several times before the lock clicked and one of the Sisters peeked out the door.

"Please let me in!" Concepcion begged. "The murderers are after us!"

The Sister swung the door wide open. "Come in, my dear. Come in, quickly."

Concepcion hurried in, clutching the baby tightly. "I need help," she cried.

"Come into the dining room, the Sister said. "Fr. Stanley will be here momentarily. "Let me get you a cup of hot coffee." They hurried into the hall.

The side door opened, and Fr. Stanley hurried in.

"Padre!" Concepcion rushed forward. "They have taken Gaspar and I know they have killed him," she screeched. "Oh, God help us. We will never find him." She broke down in tears.

Fr. Stanley held her close as grief swallowed the small women. For what seemed forever, Concepcion cried and wept in profound sorrow. "Why? She finally said. "Why Gaspar? My husband was a good man. Never a revolutionary, or guerilla. He would never fight with anyone. Gaspar never expressed his political opinions. He was good to the core."

"Why? Because he was doing the Lord's work," Stanley said. "The Lord remembers the death of his own."

***

Long after the nun had taken Concepcion and her baby back to the rest area, Fr. Stanley sat alone thinking about what was happening. There was no question but that the military had gone after Gaspar Cuban Yataz because he was one of the major voices that the locals heard on the radio every day. They had made their first strike to shut down the radio station. The attack had been well planned and deliberate. Step-by-step, the military would be taking over the town and striking the church.

Any questions that had lingered in Stanley's mind were now answered. Regardless of whatever level of propaganda the president had propagated, the church was under full-scale attack and would be so. The missionary compound had become the enemy's number one target. The war was on.

43

Sister Anna came into the early morning breakfast and sat across from Fr. Stan. She ate quietly for several minutes before she spoke. Finally, she said, "Do you think we will find Gaspar Yataz?"

The priest ran his hands nervously through his hair. "I don't expect that we will. The murderers are professional killers. He was probably buried out in some field. More of these killings will happen."

Sister Anna kept looking down at her plate. "You know what the problem is? You speak excellent Tz'utujil. The natives understand you completely. You translated the New Testament into their language. You built a hospital, a school, and a radio station for them. There aren't many foreigners who can do what you did. Consequently, the military and the government fear you. Because you are fluent, they know you can put ideas in the Indian's heads."

"I never talk politics with the natives. In fact, about all I've ever done is promote the Word of God."

"That makes no difference to the government. They want to control the people and they are afraid that you will stand in the way. So, they call you a Communist sympathizer."

"I'm afraid you are right."

"Now, we have discovered another problem," Sister Anna said. "There are growing divisions among the people. Jealousy is developing over how a few people are being treated. The military promotes these conflicts for their own purpose. I'm afraid the friction could become dangerous."

"We must work to understand what these conflicts are about," Fr. Stan concluded. "We've got to keep our ears open."

The door flew open, and Juan Mendoza rushed in. "They broke into the radio station last night!" He dropped down on the bench, trying to catch his breath. "The three guards barely escaped when the attack came. Knowing what happened to Gaspar Yataz, they ran rather than getting killed. As best we can tell, the thieves rifled through the files and stole some of the material. They took typewriters and four recorders. The station is a mess. I'm sure they disabled our equipment."

"Just as I thought," Fr. Stanley said. "Their first objective has been to disable our ability to broadcast. Looks like they are accomplishing their goal."

"After what's happened, several of our leaders have left the area. They quietly cross Lake Atitlan or sneak down the road at night. People know the government is after us."

Stanley nodded. "We will open the church at night to give sanctuary to anyone running from the government. I think the military will respect the church and leave anyone inside alone. We'll see."

***

Two days had passed since the attack on the radio station; the situation remained tense. Fewer people walked the streets. The people went way out of their way to avoid the military. Soldiers with submachine guns were everywhere. Santiago Atitlan looked like a captured city in a war zone. The Church tried to go about business as usual, but people kept disappearing.

Juan Mendoza returned to the rectory in the afternoon. "I have learned a number of important things," he told Padre Francisco. "Some of the people have become informers. They are giving names to the military."

"Do you know who they are?"

"I have learned a few of the names. The people generally know, but many are afraid to talk."

"Do you know how the informants operate?" Fr. Stanley asked.

"The government is paying the informers to talk. With so many poor people everywhere, money loosens their tongues. The average farmer only makes $50 a year anyway. They no longer have to work in the fields. The betrayers just sit around and watch. Then, they give names to the military. I have learned that there are now three different groups of deceivers, but there are conflicts between these people. The government knows how to play them against each other for their own purposes." Juan Mendoza took a deep breath. "But I tell you when names are turned in, those people are simply dead.

"Can we do anything?"

"I am collecting the names of these people who sell us out for money," Mendoza said. "When this is all over, we will know who has betrayed us. Padre Aplas, they are watching you. I know they will come asking you for this or that, only to be checking on you. You remain one of their prime targets."

"I know." Stanley shook his head. "I know."

"What are we going to do tonight."

"I have decided to leave the doors unlocked so they don't tear the wooden doors apart. I have already put the typewriters and money boxes in the safe. I will sleep with my shoes on. If I hear them coming, I will lock myself in the bathroom."

Juan Mendoza shook his head. "That way may not be enough."

"Of course, I will defend myself if attacked," Fr. Stanley said. "My friend, our hope is in the God who created the heavens and the earth. We must look at this present conflict as a challenge to our faith. We must not shrink back in fear but stand strong in our convictions. Can you do that Juan?"

The native looked fearful. "Well, I … a … never looked at the situation like that. I … I ... hope I can stand strong."

"Sure you can," the Priest said. "We must remember that these days have come only to try our faith. Keep your eyes on the Lord Jesus. He is our salvation."

"I will try," Juan said. "But it is not easy."

"Of course, that's our challenge."

Juan Mendoza nodded and hurried away.

44

Father Stanley heard the noise of someone walking in. He set his coffee cup down on the dining table cautiously. Since no one was expected, he turned toward the door with apprehension. Uninvited guests could be a sign of danger and he wasn't taking any chances. He looked toward the rear door to make sure it wasn't locked. A quick dash out the back might be necessary.

The front door opened. Fr. Pedro Bocel walked in.

"Pedro!" Stanley exclaimed. "What are you doing back here?"

Smiling broadly, the native priest walked confidently toward the table, "Gave it some thoughts and decided that I couldn't run. If you're staying, then I'm staying. That's all there is to it."

"Well son of a gun! You didn't have to come back."

"I know, but I thought about why you were staying, and I knew that was the faithful thing to do. So, here I am."

"But . . . but you must realize how dangerous everything has become."

"Sure I do, but that has nothing to do with my decision. You said the good shepherd doesn't run. I want to be the same."

Fr. Stanley shook his head. "Bless you, Pedro. Okay you're here for the long haul. We'll go on together. Sit down and let's talk"

The side door opened, and Sister Anna rushed in. "This just came. The military has called a meeting of all the religious in the area. Don't know what it's about but sounds ominous." She handed the envelope to Fr. Stanley.

He glanced at the note. "Well, Fr. Bocel. Looks like we'll be going to a meeting this afternoon.

***

The town hall room looked like the building had been there a thousand years ... maybe 500 for certain. Time hadn't been a friend to the dirty, worn adobe walls. The smell of countless events from over the centuries still hung in the air. In the small assembly room chairs had been set up in orderly rows, but only a few were filled. Fr. Stanley and Bocel took seats in the middle. A few nuns from other areas showed up. Other men walked in. Stanley knew the Wycliffe Bible Translators, but not most of the other attendees. No one said anything, but everyone looked tense.

A military officer in full uniform walked in briskly. He nodded stiffly and began at once in Spanish. He stopped and eyed Stanley. "Father Rother, you speak the native language fluently. Please translate my Spanish into the Tz'utuijil dialect as you do in Santiago Atitlan where your Church of the Apostle James is located.

The officer is trying to intimidate me, Stanley thought. *His apparent knowledge of my background is meant to make him look omniscient. Let's see if I can outsmart him.*

Stanley turned to Fr. Bocel and whispered. "Translate into Tz'utuijil what he just said. Speak up."

Fr. Bocel instantly spoke the native language.

The military officer blinked several times and looked puzzled like he didn't grasp what was going on. When Fr. Bocel finished, the officer continued with a long, winding dissertation about how the military had come to their area to protect them against the insurgents. He kept saying their purpose was to protect the people. The officer continued looking back and forth between Fr. Stanley and Fr. Bocel as if he remained confused.

When he came to the end of is prepared speech, the officer asked if there were any questions. Fr. Stanley's hand immediately shot up.

"You say that you are here to protect the people," Stanley said "However, before you came, we had peace and order. Now, every day two or three people disappear. How is it that you say you are bringing stability when our native peoples keep getting killed?"

The officer's face turned red. "Would you rather be facing formal charges?" he blurted out.

"I am only repeating what we hear on the street every day," Fr. Stanley answered.

The officer returned to is script and tried to maintain his composure. A few other questions were asked, and the meeting ended. Fr. Stanley immediately went forward and shook the officer's hand.

"Thank you for inviting us," Fr. Stanley said with a big smile.

The officer looked up at him with an uncertain stare. Maybe, he had not expected any questions. Probably, the man didn't anticipate a confrontation. He nodded perfunctorily and turned to the next person.

Fr. Stanley and Bocel started out of the town hall. Several people smiled to show their appreciation for his questions. The officer hadn't fooled most of the audience.

After they got outside the town hall, Pedro Bocel turned to Stanley. "That was a courageous thing you did, but you can bet that officer will have your number."

"I wanted him to know that we are keeping count. Every one of those murdered victims remain important to us and we will not forget anyone. I wanted to make sure that the officer got the picture. We are not intimidated," Fr. Stanley said. "They may be in control, but we stand with the Lord and in the end that is what counts the most. I wanted that officer to know that God Almighty keeps count on his own and someday the military will pay for those killings"

Fr. Bocel grinned. "You know ... you may speak softly most of the time, but underneath you are a piece of granite.

45

During the days that followed, important adjustments had to be made. The military clearly knew about the influence of the church in Santiago Atitlan. No chances could be taken. The radio station had been closed and most of the equipment taken out so it could not be stolen. All religious education classes were cancelled, and few people were on the streets. Farmers were staying out of the fields, and many were simply laying low.Fr. Pedro Bocel walked into the parish office and sat down. "I noticed that people are drawing their water extra early to get out of the way. Weren't many people out there gathering firewood either."

"Getting a little tight around here," Fr. Stanley answered. "I guess the word got around from our town hall meeting how the army claimed they are here to just help the people. Interesting that the natives are running for shelter to avoid being helped"

Fr. Bocel shrugged. "Everyone knows the truth. The military isn't fooling anybody. The villagers spread the stories of the *desaparesidos,* the local citizens, who never made it home. The body of a boy was just found and buried." He shook his head. "Happens every day."

"I think we must start changing where we sleep at night. Mixing up our schedules and locations could be helpful if someone broke in."

Pedro Bocel laughed. "You don't miss a lick, Padre Francisco."

"I just received a report that ten men went missing from the village last night. I must go out looking for them. Want to come along?"

"I-I-think I'll pass."

"Then you can check on their families," Fr. Stanley said. "They are going to need food and support. We must help the survivors in every way that we can."

"I'll work on that problem," Fr. Bocel said. "I have observed that you have a special concern for the orphans and the widows."

"The Epistle of St. James says that practical distribution of care in a time of need is the expression of a true faith. Widows and orphans must be our immediate concern. Yes, I know that we must help in every way we can even if we have to provide for them out of our own pocket."

"Which you have done," Fr. Bocel said. "Okay. I am on my way to see what I can find out there in the village. You must be more than cautious in your search."

Fr. Stanley only nodded.

***

As December 1980 approached, reports began to circulate in Oklahoma that the MICATOKLA endeavor might be flirting with Left-Wing elements. Letters flew back and forth with outrageous charges that hurt the work of the mission, but the attacks by people with political agendas didn't stop. These groups tended to believe that a benevolent Guatemalan government was being attacked by Communists elements. While Fr. Stanley knew that charges about his work were nonsense, he wanted to get the truth out.

Former workers at the mission as well as people like Jude Pansini testified to the truth. Father Adan Garcia made it clear that Fr. Stanley had never been involved with the guerilla element. Finally in his Christmas letter to the Tulsa and Oklahoma City Dioceses, Fr. Stanley wrote:

I am sure that many of you have heard rumors and saw articles about our area during the past month or two. Some are true, sad to say some exaggerated, some false, and some that haven't been told. The purported reason for the presence of the army in our immediate area is to drive out and protect us from communist guerillas. But there aren't any around here. ...

This is one of the reasons I am staying in the face of physical harm. The shepherd cannot run at the first sign of danger. Pray for us that we may be a sign of the love of Christ for our people, that our presence among them will fortify them to endure the sufferings in preparation for the coming of the kingdom. ....

Fr. Stanley could only hope the readers back in the United States could grasp the critical nature of the struggle in Guatemala. The last thing that he wanted was to be caught in a political debate back in America. There were enough deadly problems in the mission to worry about without political hotheads spouting off their errant opinions. The abductions continued everywhere across Santiago Atitlan.

***

Diego Quic knew the mission well. The Tz'utujil native had worked around the church filling many positions. He and his wife Jumana had two sons who lived in the Xechivoy canton. Diego had become one of the most sought-after catechists by the military because of his prominence in the entire community. When he sought refuge in the church, Fr. Stanley gave him a key to the rectory so he could seek sanctuary. Diego knew his name was on the death list. Knowing he would find sanctuary; he had run to the church to escape his attackers. He was within fifteen feet of the rectory when three men cut him off.

"*Ayudante!*" Diego screamed. "Somebody, help me!"

Inside the rectory. Fr. Pedro Bocel heard the scream and rushed out. He immediately realized they would attack him next. Fr. Bocel turned and ran back inside to get Stanley's help.

Fr. Stanley ran outside just as three men loaded Diego into a car. The car's engine roared to life. Stan stopped, knowing that if he rushed the car, they would shoot him. He couldn't stop the car anyway.

"They covered his mouth with a rag, a muffler of some sort," Fr. Bocel said. "But we all heard the screams."

"I'm going to call the police," Fr. Stanley said. "Probably won't change anything but we've got to try." He rushed inside and called the police station in San Lucas. "Kidnappers are headed your way!" he barked into the telephone. "In a black car! Three men kidnapped a man named Diego Quic! Please watch for them."

"Si," the officer said. "We will but they have probably already hidden."

"Do your best," Fr. Stanley said and hung up the phone. "If people in America only knew," he mumbled to himself. "Only knew the full truth."

46

When Frankie Williams came as a volunteer to help with the mission, her presence was a comfort to Fr. Stanley as he struggled with the loss of Diego Quic. The entire staff felt the pain of the abduction, but no one did like Stanley. Still, the kidnapping made it clear that Frankie needed to be on the next airplane out of Guatemala. The two friends talked while Fr. Stanley drove down the long road to the airport.

"Do you think you can tell our stories back in America?" Stanley asked.

"You bet!" Frankie answered dogmatically. "I will tell about these murderous deeds everywhere."

"We are enduring such evil attacks here that the distortions must not be allowed to stand." He pulled up to the curb in front of the La Aurora Airport.

"Don't worry, my friend. I will get the word out."

Fr. Stanley waved and drove off.

At that moment a caravan of military trucks was driving from Santiago Atitlan to Santa Clara La Laguna when a mine exploded, wrecking the truck. Soldiers leaped out and began shooting in every direction. Indians in the vicinity were mowed down with rapid fire machine guns. The soldiers killed anyone in sight.

The military rushed into the fields and began killing the farmers. Another platoon ran into three of the coffee bean areas and shot everyone dead. San Antonio Chacaya, the town closest by, got hit hard. Town dogs began barking wildly as nearly one-hundred soldiers ran down the street. People were grabbed and shoved against the walls. Men were herded like animals into the streets. Immediately the interrogations began. Some men were beaten, others killed on the spot. When men fell to the ground, the soldiers beat them with their gun butts, hitting them in the head or in their mouths while the soldiers stood on top of their bodies. The military turned torture into a ritual. Once the gruesome ordeal was finished, the bleeding and battered men were executed. Tz'utuijil fishermen dropped to the bottom of their wooden boats to disappear under their nets, but the soldiers rushed the docks and found them. After any possible information was extracted from them, they were killed. The tortured were found strewn along the shores of Lake Atitlan.

Called The Duck Massacre, the incident would later be investigated by the United Nations. As night followed, the bloody bodies were brought into the municipal plaza in Santiago Atitlan and laid out side by side. The soldiers walked around suspiciously watching what the women did. For a wife to identify her husband's body was to make her appear suspicious in the eyes of the soldiers. The simple act of claiming a loved one had become a dangerous act.

Fr. Stanley watched the hesitation and then as a widow walked forward, he stood with her when she identified her husband. The soldiers eyed him intently. One after another, Fr. Stanley stood with the widows as they filed past the bodies. Most of the women were paralyzed by grief and couldn't move.

"Padre Francisco, what shall we do?" one of the natives asked.

"I will point out seven bodies that we can bring to the church. I'll buy caskets for them to be buried in. Let's start moving them to the plaza in front of the church."

The men of the church began the long walk.

***

A week later Fr. Stanley drove to a meeting of the religious in the Diocese of Sololá. The Sisters and priests from the area gathered, knowing what had happened on the road to Santa Clara La Laguna. Tension was so thick that the participants almost felt smothered by dread hovering everywhere. The meeting began in the usual routine manner.

Finally, Fr. Stanley Rother stood up. "My dear friend and associate Diego Quic was kidnapped right in front of our rectory and before my very eyes. Then the killings exploded on the road to Santa Clara La Laguna. We are surrounded by mass murder. Are we going to sit by and do nothing? I maintain that we must do something ... something ... anything! We must protest these killings."

Silence fell over the room. No one moved. Awkwardness settled over the group.

"Can't we make a protest?" Stanley begged. "Aren't we willing to make these murderers known?"

No one moved. Finally, a Maryknoll Sister raised her hand. "We could raise some money."

Father Stanley stared at her, almost not believing what he heard. "Money? Are you kidding?"

Once more, silence.

By the time the meeting ended, Bishop Melotto found himself in the awkward position of being forced to decide. Fr. Stanley's blunt request had forced the issue. He declined, fearing that a forceful response would only bring more persecution on the Indians. The participants dispersed but it was clear that the reign of terror had a tight grip on the majority.

Fr. Stanley left the meeting with a biting sense of consternation. Even the religious had been intimidated by the government. As he reflected on the bishop's meeting, a sense of loneliness settled over him. The next day he was leaving for Guatemala City when a friend in the village hailed him down.

"Listen to me carefully," the native said. "The military have put you and Father Bocel on the list to kill. Both of you are in grave danger. You must act immediately. Believe me, Padre Francisco. This action is imminent."

Fr. Stanley immediately called his old friend Fr. Gregory Schaffer to meet him at the American Embassy. They had to get a U.S. residency visa for Father Pedro. If they didn't, he was dead.

47

For sixteen days, the two priests were shuffled around the countryside and kept hidden. When the visa for Pedro Bocel was approved, both men rushed straight to the airport and flew out of the country with Stanley escorting Pedro to safety. When Fr. Stanley got off the airplane in Oklahoma City, Gertrude rushed forward and kissed her son. For the moment, he had escaped the gun. She could hardly contain herself.

During his brief time in Oklahoma, Stanley met with old friends, school classmates, and spoke on the mission. He passionately presented the challenge in Santiago Atitlan the church faced. There was no question that he was going back as soon as the tension subsided somewhat.

In April 1981, Fr. Stanley flew back to Guatemala. To check out the conditions in the country, he first went to the American Embassy to speak with Ray Gonzales, a political officer at the Embassy who was trusted by the missionaries. Gonzales warned him that it was too dangerous to return to Santiago Atitlan. When he left the Embassy, Fr. Stanley went to see Bishop Angelico Moletto. Again, Stan was warned that it was too treacherous to return to Santiago Atitlan. The number of soldiers around the city had doubled from 300 to 600 men. His response remained the same. "My life is for my people. I am not scared."

Despite the warning signs, life in the mission seemed rather calm. The few remaining workers went about their business with few interruptions. Holy Week came and went with no problems. Nevertheless, tension hung in the air.

The annual celebration and feast of St. James the Apostle always came on July 25. Even with concern and worry permeating the event, a record high of 101 couples witnessed their marriages and 200 received their first Communion. Nothing stopped the work of the parish.

Nevertheless, the fiesta felt like a volcano about to explode. Soldiers with automatic weapons cruised through the crowds. A Sister always walked with Fr. Stanley when he stopped and talked with the people. The attendance had dropped dramatically.

"*Como estas?*" Stanley asked a little woman with a baby. She forced a smile and held up the baby. He walked on with the Sister standing close by his side.

The natives could not help but notice that some of the soldiers kept their weapons pointed at the rectory. As the fiesta ended, so did some of the mission's routines. The Sisters began sleeping with their passports under their pillows. During the group's prayer times, their involvement in intercession became intense. Sometimes after prayer, the group would play a game or have some sort of recreation to lighten everybody up. Never once did Father Stanley miss celebrating the Mass. He simply kept going.

Fr. Stanley travelled to Cerro de Oro for his final Mass with the community he had diligently served for a long time. In his homily, he urged the people to be constant and to keep the faith under all circumstances. He urged them to follow the Word of God. As the service ended, the people surged forward to thank Stanley for his service. Emotion flowed freely both from the people and the priest.

Back in the sacristy, Fr. Stanley removed his stole and prepared to take off his alb. Manuel Ajcahul Lacan, the lay president of the parish, walked in softly. "May I speak to you?"

Fr. Stanley turned, "Manuel! My old friend, most certainly."

"Before you came to our village, we struggled with chaos and confusion. Often, the people became angry with each other. We had no spiritual guidance for a long, long time. Then you came. I cannot tell you what a difference your presence has made. Even with the problem of the military, stability and hope has come back to Cerro de Oro."

"What you are describing is the work of Christ that comes through the Mass," Fr. Stanley explained. "Jesus Christ imparts hope and the blessed promise of eternal life. Faith in those facts changes people. This is what has made the difference in your town."

"Yes," Manuel said. "Most true. But you brought that message. You have been the conveyer of the promises. We can never thank you enough."

Father Stanley smiled. "Thank you. Your kind words will always remain as an encouragement to me."

The president of the parish wiped a tear from his eye, turned, and hurried away. A young man stepped in. "I have a message for you, Padre. You should go by the village of San Lucas on your way home. Father Adan Garcia sends a plea for you stop and talk with him."

"Ah, my old associate! Father Garcia is a dear friend. Sure. I'll go immediately."

***

Father Adan had been with the St. James Parish years earlier but always remained a dear friend and comrade in the ministry. The dirt road proved to be like all the back roads: bumpy and full of potholes. Stan knew he had to pay careful attention to keep from hitting a chug hole that could really damage the vehicle. When he turned the final corner of the dusty old road and turned into the village, he pulled up in front of the rectory that looked like it needed a few repairs.

"Buenos tardes!" Stanley called out when he pulled up to the driveway and got out.

Fr. Garcia had been sitting on the porch as if doing nothing but waiting for him to come. He waved and said, *"Acceder al poder ."*

The two friends walked into the front room and sat down at a small table in one corner.

"How about a nice glass of wine?" Fr. Garcia said. "You've already put in a good day's work."

"Sounds good to me," Stanley said. "How's the ministry of the parish going?"

"You know how it is. People are scared, frightened. We are living in a most difficult time."

Fr. Stanley nodded. "Never has our witness been more vitally needed. We are helping the people to stand fast."

"That is what I wanted to talk with you about," Fr. Adan said. "I have some important political connections that are highly reliable. I have learned that the government has decided to kill you. If you

- 258 -

want to live, you cannot go back to Santiago Atitlan. I know that you had many warnings in the past, but what I have learned is final. You must leave the country."

Fr. Stanley leaned back in his chair and took a long sip of the red wine. "I appreciate your concern and resources. I have thought about this situation for a long time. I must tell you that I have already come to my Gethsemane. I know that the military could have killed me a long time ago, but for providential reasons, they did not attack me. What you are telling me is that maybe time has now run out."

"I am afraid so, my dear friend. I don't want to lose you."

"Thank you, and that means more than I can say. I must tell you that I have decided that my life is in His hands. If the end is at hand, then let it be so."

"Listen to me," Adan pleaded. "Get your passport and I can get you out of the country."

"My friend, I have made a commitment to the people and to the Sisters. I will not leave the parish. The government cannot drive me out. If the end comes, then I am ready."

"The military has been merciless. They torture the people they capture."

Stanley forced a smile. "Don't worry. I will fight if they try to take me. They won't take me alive."

48

Monday arrived with the usual demands that always followed the large celebration of Sunday Mass with the natives crowding into St. James Church. As always Fr. Stanley celebrated the Mass but seemed more emotional than usual. Still, Monday came again sending everyone scurrying to care for their responsibilities.

Fr. Stanley had just sat down at his desk in his office when Christobal Coche Ajtzip walked in. The villager had been hired earlier to be a night watchman. For two years, he had maintained oversight over the rectory and all the adjoining property.

"Padre Francisco," Christobal began, "my second son really had a hard time yesterday. He has been battling illness all weekend. My boy is very sick."

"I'm sorry to hear that," Fr. Stanley said. "Has he been taken to the hospital?"

"We are going to do so today," Ajtzip explained. "I am sure that this means I will not be able to make the rounds tonight."

"Oh? Tonight?"

"I am most sorry, but my wife has been up with the boy all weekend and now I must take my turn. We fear for his life."

"Hmm, not the best time to be absent, but you must help your family. No question about that responsibility."

"Please, Padre. May I be frank with you?"

"Of course."

"The rumor going around the town is that the army will try to kill you tonight."

Fr. Stanley shrugged. "I've heard that many times. The military spreads those rumors to frighten the people. I no longer worry about such reports. You must do for your son what is necessary. Don't worry about me."

"But I do."

"I am not afraid of death," Stanley said. "Just remember to intercede for me."

Christobal Coche Ajtzip rolled his eyes. "I can only pray you are correct, and no one comes." He bowed his head and walked out.

"Bless you," Fr. Stanley called after him.

***

As he always did, Fr. Stanley celebrated the 5:00 p.m. Mass. After he finished, Sister Rosa Valentina and Sister Herlinda Yos accompanied him down to the city market. They joined the people shopping among the stalls and up and down the lane. The crowd could be large.

"I think we need some bananas." Stanley moved down several stalls, looking carefully at the produce.

"Also some grapes," Sister Rosa said and pointed to a small pile of apples. "They look excellent."

"Just a minute," Fr. Stanley said. "Did you notice people moving away from us."

Sister Herlinda nodded. "We seem to be clearing out the market just by walking through. People are leaving."

Fr. Stanley walked up to one of the proprietors that he'd known for a long time. "What's going on?" he whispered.

The man looked up and down the street before he spoke and then leaned closer. "The army is cruising through the town picking up young men to force them to become soldiers. Our men are running into hiding. No one is getting close to anyone. People know the military is after you. Every move is watched because everything has become unpredictable."

"I understand," Stanley said slowly. "People are running for cover." He walked away.

"What did you learn?" Sister Rosa asked.

"We must return to the church. I anticipate I will have my own army waiting for me asking to use the church for sanctuary."

Both Sisters agreed. "We must hurry."

Winding their way out of the marketplace, the three took side streets. Without slowing they soon came out on the plaza in front of St. James Church.

"Look at that assembly waiting by the church's front door," Sister Herlinda said. "That's a lot of guys."

"Just what I thought," Fr. Stanley said. "They are running from the military.

With long strides, the priest hurried to the front of the group of men standing on the steps. He scurried up through the crowd and unlocked the front door.

"Listen to me!" the priest shouted. "Everyone who comes inside the church has sanctuary, protection. You must be quiet and reverent. So far, the army has honored our helping people and not attacked us. I cannot guarantee what they will do, but I believe you'll be okay."

"This is so much better than being hauled away and forced to kill people!" a young man shouted. "You have saved us!"

The group applauded and shouted their praise. The young men rushed forward and hurried inside. Fr. Stanley stood by the door and watched. When he glanced across the plaza, the priest saw two soldiers standing in one of the street entrances and watching the young men going into the church. They would surely report to their superiors what they had observed.

***

The evening proved to be typical. The staff sat around talking about the day, chatting, sharing stories. The group always enjoyed being together. Sometimes they played games or danced.

"Did you hear that?" one of the Sisters asked. "That pounding noise? Sounded like someone trying to break in."

"Yes!" Sister Anne added. "I think someone could be climbing over the wall between the church and the rectory. Let's check."

Fr. Stanley led the way. When he opened the outside room, he found three young men standing there. "What are you doing?"

"Please, Padre Francisco, don't turn us away." the first boy said.

"If the soldiers catch us, they will make us become one of them," the second boy said.

"We need sanctuary," the third boy said.

Fr. Stanley looked at the boys and then back at the two Sisters. "Should we let them in?" He grinned.

"Of course!" Sister Anne said. "Naturally."

"Okay, boys," Fr. Stanley said. "The Sisters will take you upstairs where you can sleep tonight. Tomorrow, we will take you over to the church."

"*Oh, gracias!*" the three boys exclaimed at once. "*Gracias! Gracias!*"

They all walked back inside, and Stanley locked the door behind them. The staff's conversations continued until around 10:20. Everyone agreed it had been a long, trying day and it was time to turn in. Stanley walked to the room where he would sleep and locked the door behind him.

***

The cool of the night had settled around the parish. At about 1:30 that morning the sound of wood breaking echoed through the rectory. Some of the staff stirred, but most slept. The noise grew louder as three men rushed up the steps to the bedrooms. They obviously knew exactly where they were going. Throwing their body weight against the door to Fr. Stanley's room, they forced the door open.

The first man shined his flashlight on the bed. "What? There's nobody here?"

"We were told this is where he'd be here!"

"He's moved to a different room!" one of the men yelled.

The men rushed down the hall and kicked open the next door. A young man sat up in bed.

"Who are you?" one of the intruders growled.

"F-Francisco B-Bocel," the boy stammered. Pedro Bocel ... the associate priest ... is my brother."

The second gunman crammed a pistol in Francisco's face. "I am going to blow your head off if you don't tell me where the Padre is...*right now!*"

"Please ... please, don't shoot."

"Where is the priest? Start showing us. NOW!"

Francisco stumbled out of bed. One of the men grabbed him by the hair and pushed him toward the door. The young man staggered down the stairs and stopped near the bottom. He pointed toward the corner utility room. The three men rushed to the door and beat on it.

Francisco yelled, "Padre, they've come for you!"

The lock clicked and the door cracked open slightly and the priest stared through the narrow space. The entry opened slightly wider. "Francisco, go back upstairs to your room," the priest ordered. "Run!"

The first man pushed the door wide open. "We're taking you with us."

"I don't think so," Stanley hit him in the face with all his strength.

The man tumbled backward on the floor. Francisco Bocel broke away and dashed up the stairs.

The second man rushed Stanley and they flew back into the room. The sound of furniture breaking and bodies crashing into the wall echoed through the entire rectory. Abruptly, a gunshot roared through the complex. Then a second shot exploded followed by the sound of men rushing out of the building.

An eerie silence settled over the rectory.

49

The sound of boots running across the plaza no longer echoed. Francisco Bocel listened until he was sure the three attackers were gone and then leapt out from behind the door screaming, "They killed him! They killed our Padre Francisco!" The young man dashed outside the rectory screeching, "They've killed our priest!"

Up and down the stairs of the rectory, the staff leaped out of bed and began running through the rooms. The Sisters ran from the convent to the rectory. Lights went on around the property. The staff knew where Padre Francisco slept that night. They ran for the room.

Young Bocel stood outside the hall pointing to the open door. "Help! The army has attacked! They murdered him!"

The Sisters rushed in and found the door to Fr. Stanleys room wide open. They knelt beside his body, weeping and praying. Surrounding his head was an ever-widening pool of blood. One of the Sisters had gauze and tried to place it on the wound on Stanley's jaw, but the dressing did little good. The second bullet had entered his left temple and gone completely through his head, lodging in the far wall. There was nothing that the nurses could do. Finally, Bertha Sanchez, a nurse volunteer, felt for Stanley's pulse.

"He gone," she said and wept.

"Look at his hand," Sister Rosa said. "The skin is gone from his knuckles. He must have clobbered his assailant."

"There is blood over all the walls," another Sister noticed. "Must have been a terrible fight."

"The murderers assaulted Father's body," Bertha added. "You can see the stab wounds through his T-shirt and pants. I think he must have been gone before they knifed him."

"Fr. Stanley's arm is still raised as if he were defending himself," Sister Rosa said. "The struggle must have been fierce and awful. We must save the bloody gauze and as much of his blood as we can. I will run into the kitchen and see if I can find empty jars. I know there was a peanut butter jar and another large container there the other night."

"Hurry," Berta said. "We will wait for your return."

"All we can do now is pray," Carmelite Sister Maria whispered.

***

The word spread like wildfire. All around Lake Atitlan, the people heard and fell into mourning. Shock and grief spread like an infection. The natives descended into deep grief and despair. Fr. Stanley Rother had stood with them, defended them, and been their true friend when the government turned on their tribe. Father had been the only true friend they could count on. They loved him and could hardly bare his death.

Because Stanley had been so tall, none of the caskets fit him. A special long-length wooden frame had to be quickly constructed. The workman immediately went to construct the long container made from wood donated by the local natives.

The owner turned to his associate who worked with him in the funeral shop. "You know ... Padre Francisco had a face like St. Francis. That countenance was reflected in his name."

"And Padre had love and dedication like Christ," the helper added. The two men went back to work, laboring silently, saying nothing more.

The Carmelite Sisters had taken Fr. Stanley's body to the hospital. After preparing him, they dressed him in a chasuble and laid on his shoulders the *cofradia's* shawl that he had been so proud to wear. Unfortunately, the bullet had distorted his face.

"Father told me that he wanted Resurrection songs sung at his funeral," the Sister said. "When we were decorating the sanctuary for Easter, he emphasized that resurrection hymns were the theme he wanted in his funeral."

"And such shall be," the Carmelite Sister mumbled solemnly.

The day of the funeral, the church was packed shoulder-to-shoulder. The benches had been removed to allow more space. Tz'utujil natives walked in wearing the best traditional clothing they had. The people strained forward to be as near the coffin as possible.

A solemn procession began marching down the center aisle with Fr. Rother's casket held on the men's shoulders. Two large jars that contained his blood and a metal box containing the martyr's heart were in the procession. As the coffin was placed near the front, the two jars were set in the center of the altar, a reminder that the faithful priest's heart would always remain with his people.

A little old Indian woman knelt at the end of one of the pews when the casket was carried by. She wailed, "They killed our priest… He was my priest. … He spoke our language …" Her voice trailed away.

The coffin was lowered in the center of the front of the sanctuary. The congregants broke into song. They sang with a forcefulness that broke through the walls of the church and floated out over the overflow crowd standing on the plaza. The faith of the mourners merged with the hymn's promise, "He who believes in me shall never die … I am the bread of life … and will lift him up at the last day …" a promise each of the Indians claimed for themselves. At that moment, the murmuring of the congregation drowned out the words of the celebrant. All across the 2,000-member congregation people kept repeating, "Padre Francisco … Padre Aplas … Padre Francisco…"

At the end of the service, the congregation began to file passed the coffin. Many reached out to touch the wood as if they could made one final contact with their beloved priest. The line filed out of the exit into the plaza where more mourners had gathered. Finally, Fr. Stanley's body was loaded in an ambulance that drove slowly through Santiago Atitlan. Along the way, people pressed against the vehicle saying goodbye to their friend.

"Where are they going?" one of the bystanders asked Sister Rosa.

"They are going to the airport in Guatemala City. Father Stanley's family has allowed his heart to remain with his people here, but his body will be returned to Oklahoma to be buried in the family cemetery in Okarche, Oklahoma."

"Okarche?" the bystander said. "What a strange name?"

Sister Rosa forced a smile. "A strange name? In a land of impossible names? I guess so."

"You were his friend?"

"Even now with this massive crowd, we feel lonely. Like the Bible says, we have become like sheep without a shepherd." Her face grimaced. "We will miss our good shepherd more than I can tell you." Sister Rosa walked away with her head down.

50

Five Years Later

Padre Clemente Penelen had just finished celebrating the Mass and returned to the sacristy in Santiago Atitlan's St. James the Apostle Church. The jet black-haired son of the parish, a full blooded Tz'utujil native, carefully laid the chasuble across the tabletop and folded his stole.

"Five years to the day," his associate Antonio Cruz said. "Hard to believe that Fr. Stanley was assassinated on this very day. I believe he will be officially proclaimed a martyr by the Vatican. If not, Fr. Stanley should be."

"We put his wooden casket in the front of the sanctuary because our people are always so moved by it. Of course, he had to be transferred to a different container for transfer back to America, but we keep that coffin sacred. You know, I became a priest because of the kindness Padre Francisco showed me when I was just a boy."

"Yes, I know he really helped you," the associate said "I went to the place of his death that is now a chapel. The bullet hole in the wall has been well perservered. His picture on the little altar confronts one with the challenge that his life gave us. His blood is now encased in a glass with a handwritten sign underneath:

SANGRE DE APLAS, EL 28 DE JULIO DE 1981. Many people go there to pray all the time."

Padre Clemente Penelen nodded. "Yes, you know Sister Linda Wanner brings people from the United States on a pilgrimage here every year. Other people continually arrive throughout the year. People are coming just as they once did to other holy sites. I know that Rome has not made it official yet, but our people are calling him Saint Stanley. Of course, there must be verifiable miracles by him for the church to confirm that claim, but I feel like Father Stanley is right here watching over what we do."

"I know that the word martyr in the original Greek means a witness," Antonio said. "I think that what made Fr. Stanley such a powerful witness was that he incarnated, he embodied his testimony. He witnessed every day through acts of charity and kindness. Then in the critical moment of confrontation, he did not back down. I believe that made him a martyr for our time."

"You know when we say the creed in the Mass, we affirm that we believe in the 'communion of the saints.' That means that Fr. Stanley is still at work all the time. I believe he continues to bless us here. Moreover, he is probably working in many other places. Our brother has not stopped working"

The associate smiled. "Father Stanley would make a good saint for all priests. He served with total devotion and upheld the faith in the most difficult times. He spoke so often of how the example of St. John Vianney, the Cure d Ars, was an example for him. They had such a similar background. Both men struggled in their studies and lived in difficult times. Each maintained a concern for the poor and destitute, even giving out of their pockets to help the destitute. Quite amazing similarity."

"You know, this parish sat here for a hundred years with no clergy in sight," Padre Clemente said. "Nothing went on. Then the MICATOKLA came and eventually Fr. Stanley became our shepherd. Rather amazing that after all the struggle, warfare, and brutality to our people, now a full-blooded Tz'utujil Indian is now the parish priest. Father Stanley made that possible. No small accomplishment."

"Perhaps after a few miracles surface, we will call him St. Stanley," Antonio Cruz said.

Padre Clemente Penelen smiled. "Perhaps."

EPILOGUE

On July 27, 2022, this story was reported in Tulsa, Oklahoma on Channel 6. The same day the same account was reported in Oklahoma City.

DAILY OKLAHOMAN
Red Dirt Diaries: One Miracle

Wednesday, July 27th, 2022, 9:07 pm
By: News 9

An Oklahoma born Priest, murdered in his church, is one step away from sainthood. That one step though is a BIG one: he needs to be credited with a miracle. We talked to one metro man who says he's living proof of just that in our Red Dirt Diaries.

When you're in need of help from above who do you pray to?

Johnny Workman believes he's here today because his family answered that for him after a horrible accident in 2018.

"I felt something kind of hit me in the back and when I turned, I got trapped," he explains.

Trapped by run-away 30,000-pound asphalt roller. The weight of two elephants pinned him against the roller, crushing him.

"I saw myself in the mirror, I saw myself changing colors and then I blacked out," he says.

Workman suffered twenty-seven fractures to his chest alone. While in a medically induced coma, his family placed a medal of Blessed Stanley Rother on Workman's chest and prayed for the intercession of the Priest who grew up in Okarche.

"I believe that's when it happened- the miracle," says Workman.

Workman remains unwavering in the vision he experienced while unconscious.

"He picked me up and we were walking together- Mother Mary on one side and he was on the other. Stanley Rother grabbed me by the hand, and we were walking. [I] don't know if we were going to heaven."

Rother served his church in Guatemala during a time of civil war. Thousands of Catholics were killed. In 1981 three men entered his church and executed Father Stanley. In 2016 Pope Francis officially recognized him as a martyr for the faith putting him closer to sainthood.

"We have one more step left to go and that means a verified miracle, verified by the Vatican," explains Diane Clay with the Archdiocese of Oklahoma City.

That's one of the reasons the shrine in south OKC, which will hold Blessed Stanley's remains is opening later this year.

"Having a shrine dedicated to a person provides an opportunity and encourages people to seek his intercession right where he is," says Clay.

The Vatican has a Miracle Commission that goes through the thousands of miraculous claims. Ninety-Nine-point 9 percent are medical miracles. For it to be considered a miracle, it has to be spontaneous, instantaneous and the person needs to be completely healed with no natural explanation of what happened.

Workman describes his recovery as nothing short of miraculous.

"Doctors nurses and staff would tell me almost every day I was lucky to be alive."

A letter of his account has been delivered to the Oklahoma City Archdiocese describing his now healed body as the result of more than good luck.

"Maybe it's a miracle in the churches, but I know with 100% fact that it was a miracle in my eyes," says Workman.

--The End--